The Captive and the Prince:

TALES OF FREEDOM AND COURAGE

Including the novella previously published as
A Bride Called Freedom

Also by Brett Alan Sanders

Author

A Bride Called Freedom
(Bilingual Edition: Spanish translation by Sebastián R.Bekes)

Confabulating with the Cows

Translator

Awaiting the Green Morning (Bilingual Edition), by María Rosa Lojo
Passionate Nomads, by María Rosa Lojo
We Are All Whitman(Bilingual Edition), by Luis Alberto Ambroggio

The Captive and the Prince:

TALES OF FREEDOM AND COURAGE

Including the novella previously published as
A Bride Called Freedom

Brett Alan Sanders

Per Bastet

The Captive and the Prince: Tales of Freedom and Courage

Published by Per Bastet Publications LLC, P.O. Box 3023
Corydon, IN 47112

Cover design and art by Robert Priester

ISBN 978-1-942166-74-0

Available in trade paperback and DRM-free ebook formats

A Bride Called Freedom was previously published by Ediciones Nuevo Espacio (ENE)
Title: A Bride Called Freedom / Una novia llamada libertad
ISBN: 1-930-879-31-8

Nothing comes from nothing . . . no story comes from nowhere; new stories are born from old — it is the new combinations that make them new.

Salman Rushdie,
Haroun and the Sea of Stories

The Captive and the Prince:

TALES OF FREEDOM AND COURAGE

Including the novella previously published as
A Bride Called Freedom

Dedication

To my friends in the Southern Indiana Writers' Group,
whose help on the new story was indispensable
— and especially to my editor, Marian Allen,
who is in no small part responsible for
the revised novella's final perfections.

And to all those still struggling
for their own and for others' human dignity,
everywhere and wherever they are found.

Table of Contents

Fiction

Essays from Behind the Curtain

A Memoiristic Journey, with Digressions

Foreword

The story of how the novella “A Bride Called Freedom” came to be published as an English / Spanish bilingual book is related in the essay “In Search of Dorotea Bazán” and included immediately after these two fictional narratives. In this new edition I have made a number of small refinements to that text and a couple of larger ones, but without altering the central story in any significant way.

The seed to its new companion story, “The Prince and His Father,” actually existed in the earliest draft of what became that book. In one of several narratives originally interwoven with Dorotea’s, a mysterious roving storyteller related at length the historical-mythical tale of the Incan Empire that now appears more briefly in this new incarnation.

Its framing story is entirely new and completely contemporary, set in the United States at approximately the present historical moment. It is centered on the struggles of the young boy, Pacha, to find his place and his role in this real world that we all share. Pacha’s mother, Viviana, is the woman who, more than a decade and a half earlier, traveled from the U.S. to Argentina, discovered the manuscript containing Dorotea’s story, and told it in emails home to her best friend from high school; and who afterwards gave it all to the fictional editor who fictitiously published it, whose note appears before Viviana’s first email-chapter.

In “A Bride Called Freedom,” the framing story is secondary to the discovered tale of nineteenth-century Dorotea, captive of Indians and then of her presumed liberators. In “The Prince and His Father,” on the other hand, the main story is the modern one, while the one that Viviana narrates — set principally in the Andean highlands of Perú — is secondary to it. In other words, while in “Bride” the framing story of Viviana and her ironic intrusions serve to cast light on the interior story, in Pacha’s case it is his mother’s story-within-the-story that casts light on his exterior one. But its mystical imagery is present from beginning to end, joining myth and reality in new configurations.

Thus, by Viviana’s presence in both stories, the original Inca narrator’s tale finally finds its true place beside Dorotea’s tale of the Argentine pampas. Viviana is, in that sense, the force that unites those two universes.

In the fashion of other stories by such luminaries as Twain, Dickens, and Rowling, I hope that mine will find their audience among a diversity of readers from younger to older, adolescent or adult — without regard to the narrow, arbitrary categorizations that these days divide literatures and people.

Brett Alan Sanders
Tell City, Indiana
May, 2018 / June 2020

A Bride Called Freedom

Yo tengo tantos hermanos que no los puedo contar,
y una novia hermosa que se llama Libertad.

I have so many brothers and sisters that I can't count them,
and a beautiful bride who's called Freedom

Atahualpa Yupanqui (1908-1992),
(born Héctor Roberto Chavero Aramburu),
Argentine poet, singer, musician

Yo no soy huinca, *capitán, hace tiempo lo fui.*
Deje que vuelva para el Sur, déjeme ir allí.
Mi nombre casi lo olvidé: Dorotea Bazán.
Yo no soy huinca, *india soy, por amor, capitán.*
Me falta el aire pampa y el olor de los ranqueles campamentos,
el cobre oscuro de la piel de mi señor,
en ese imperio de gramilla, cuero y sol.
Usted se asombra, capitán, que me quiera volver,
un alarido de malón me reclama la piel.
Yo me hice india y ahora estoy más cautiva que ayer.
Quiero quedarme en el dolor de mi gente ranquel.
Yo no soy huinca, *capitán, hace tiempo lo fui.*
Deje que vuelva para el Sur, déjeme ir allí.

I'm not *winca*, captain; some time ago I was.
Let me return toward the South; let me cross over there.
I'd almost forgotten my name: Dorotea Bazán.
I'm not *winca*, captain; I'm Indian, for love.
I miss the pampa air and smell of the Ranquel encampments,
the dark copper of my husband's skin,

in that empire of rawhide, grass, and sun.
You're shocked, captain, that I would want to return;
a raider's cry is reclaiming my skin.
I became Indian and now I'm more captive than before.
I want to stay within my Ranquel people's pain.
I'm not *winca*, captain; some time ago I was.
Let me return toward the South; let me cross over there.

Félix Luna (1925-2009),
"*Dorotea la cautiva*" (Dorotea, the Captive)

For Anita —
bride of my youth,
love of my life;

And our children —
Jonathan, Nadina, Stephanie;

For being there for me through the years
of this story's long gestation

Editor's Note

These email letters were handed to me by their author herself. Viviana Suárez was an unusually gifted undergraduate student in a seminar I gave in the spring of 2002. She was a freshman and would normally have been ineligible for the class before her senior or, at the earliest, her junior year. I accepted her on the basis of these letters alone, which she presented to me in the present chaptered format. They perfectly fit our topic: the forgotten presence of women in colonial and post-colonial Latin American literature. What's more, her manuscript constituted an original contribution to the field that any one of her mostly graduate-level classmates would have died for.

Later she would show me her antique Argentine source, copied in elegant Spanish handwriting (analysis dates the ink to over a hundred years old). In her "prologue" she clarifies the circumstances surrounding this discovery; also, the existence of a poem that would seem to corroborate the story's authenticity.

Both letters and poem concern the legend of one Dorotea Bazán, said to have been captured by Indians in the late nineteenth century. While the source itself is not clear on this, Ms. Suárez suggests that she was a descendant of poor immigrants from Galicia, one of the numerous non-Castilian regions of Spain. Be that as it may, I have found the work remarkable, from the document itself to its translator's own imaginative insertions. I do not claim an absolute knowledge of what might be factual or fabricated in the core narrative, but it is grounded in a terrain at once solid and convincing.

Beyond that, I must not forget to thank my publisher, whose willingness to bring this obscure tale to light has been my consolation in these times of personal grief. Thank you, Joseph, for your immeasurable kindness.

Anna Castresana
Chair of the Department of Latino Studies
Mariposa Community College, New Mexico
July, 2005

Prologue:

Dorotea Bazán, Discovered

[December, 2000]

Dear Leeza,

I've happened on proof that she really might have existed!

Can you believe it? Señor Connor's obsession? The poem he made us recite by memory in its Argentine-accented Castilian Spanish? The sultry thickness of that woman's scratchy recording our teacher had brought home with him years earlier to help yet-future students practice their recitation? The one-act musical play that he wrote himself and cajoled the drama club into presenting before our entire school and families?

God knows you can't have forgotten, Leeza. We were sophomores then. You were his Dorotea! You sang that very song! First a chorus in Spanish: mysterious and somber, to set the proper mood. Then in Señor Connor's own adapted English. A poetic rendition, he said, not slavishly literal or else it wouldn't fit the guitar's rhythm. The guitar that he played offstage, in unseen shadows, while you, his musical protégé, dulcetly sang.

I don't think I really thought much about her at the time. Did you? As someone who might have ever been flesh-and-blood, I mean, who might have actually lived. Sure, I'd remembered reading some children's book about the Mary Jemison story back in elementary school. North America's own Dorotea. Or one of them. Miss McNamara had told us that she ended up marrying among her captors and that she loved her husband, bore him children. It wasn't that I thought it impossible. This song of a white woman captured by Indians? Arguing years later with the Argentine captain who would forcefully redeem her for "civilization"? "*Yo no soy winca, capitán,*" she's supposed to have said. "I'm not *winca* — I'm not a foreigner, not Christian — but Indian, by mystery of love." Of course it could have been true, as Señor Connor believed but could not prove. It could have been, sure. But the story, like our old teacher's obsession, struck me then as vaguely childish. Like something that might have interested me years ago but that couldn't compete with the concerns of burgeoning, turn-of-the-twenty-first-century adulthood. Besides, he'd told us himself that the story didn't exist in its alleged source. A problem that visibly troubled him.

How pleased he'll be with his former student when he learns that I've solved it! First thing when I'm back in the States, I'll stop in on him. Meanwhile let me tell you, Leeza, my good and faithful friend, how it came to be.

I owe it to my parents who allowed me the luxury of this year-long vacation between high school and university, and my paternal aunt who gave me lodging and freedom to roam in this grand metropolis where she and Papi were both raised. My aunt is a professor of literature. When I laughingly told her the story of our dear teacher's obsession, she gave me the two volumes of Lucio Mansilla's *Excursion to the Ranquel Indians* — the famous "source," according to the blurb inside that old vinyl's cover, of Dorotea's story. Of course Señor Connor was right, it wasn't there. But the narrative that I did discover absolutely (who knew?) enchanted me.

Just yesterday here in Buenos Aires it's only by the weirdest chance that I finally stumble upon what, with more enthusiasm than certainty, I'll still call "proof." Proof? That someone *might* have existed? The manuscript, though apparently ancient, quite visibly delicate, is the hand-copied shadow of an almost certainly vanished original. Is it truthful history or imitative fiction? The old woman who handed it to me had possessed it in secret for as long as she can remember. When I'd whispered to her over a sip of the national tea (that bitter yerba maté) of captive Dorotea's mystery, she rose, mysteriously. She emerged long seconds later cradling those weathered pages. She said my eyes remind her of how she's imagined Dorotea's! That I should take this before she dies and it's lost! It was an inheritance, she said, from her mother, who claimed to have it from a friend of Eduarda Mansilla de García, Lucio's sister.

Can there be another copy? If mine is the only one, how is it that the lyricist knew both name and story? While I'm still in Argentina, I should do some digging. But do I want to know? Is it perhaps nobler to just believe with pure faith, like windmill-tilting Don Quixote?

Yes: Dorotea lives! What will follow, in future letters, is her "true" history — as recounted privately to Mansilla, recorded but never published.

You must imagine, my darling Leeza, why the story might have finally taken such a hold on me. This woman, whose life now presents itself in more developed form than any previous feminine narrative of these pampas, is too much to resist. But is it history, faithfully recorded, or Mansilla's invention? Or is it in fact his sister Eduarda's story, as-told-to or fictional, masquerading behind her brother's more famous name? Or is it someone else's invention entirely?

These are all questions, Leeza, whose answers I don't pretend to know. Their clarification awaits the investigations of greater scholars than I. To me just leave the full revelation of the romance.

With affection,

Vivi

Chapter 1
In which the scene is set

Mansilla (if it is Mansilla), in allowing captive Dorotea to speak for herself, gives no space to either a physical description of her or of the setting she speaks in. Allow me, then, this bit of willful fancy.

Her captor, let's say, is the Captain Rivadavia who appears briefly in the *Excursion*; we'll have him traveling out of Ranquel country with Colonel Mansilla. Trailing them on her horse, Dorotea approaches the crest of the sandy dune. Brushing from her face her windswept, auburn hair like her Galician ancestors', she reins in the horse and gazes out at the scene below. That pond with its green water — La Verde, as it is appropriately enough called — lies nestled there in a verdant hollow. At Mansilla's barked command, his men are hastily preparing camp.

La Verde, as Mansilla will describe it, is a deep, circular pond of some three hundred meters in diameter, within a dune that reaches an elevation of about seventy feet. Its water is abundant and fresh, sweet-tasting and clean. Its shores are rich in sharp-edged, green bulrushes, yellowish cattails, and perfumed clovers. The dune, falling abruptly toward the pond at its heart, is itself rich with foliage; locust, nandubay, and chañar trees tower over fresh, pampean grasses of several varieties. The road north, forking toward Villa Mercedes to the west or Fort Sarmiento to the east, determines this welcome oasis as a natural crossroads for travelers, both Christian and Indian. Whether they're going northward or toward the untamed south is all the same.

Within the shadows of La Verde's days, within the dark of its nights, those weary travelers find both rest and refuge. Around its fires they find conversation and other lives.

It's here, dear Leeza, that I need your help. Step once more into your former role for me. Be, if you will, that Dorotea. And now, as you slip back into that remote woman's being, I'll teach her to you afresh, her secrets that our old teacher couldn't conjure. Go along now, approach the fire that's just beginning to crackle and warm. Get off your horse and stand there alone, gazing distractedly, sadly, into its flame. Look at the young captain, solitary and stubborn, where he's standing a few feet away. Stride toward him, abruptly, driven by the most sudden and urgent impulse. Look squarely into his eyes. Address him again with the words we already know.

Rivadavia sighs as you corner him there. He sits down on the horizontal prong of an enormous, dead tree. Another branch angles up at about a forty-five degree angle from the first, passing just over his head where he's sitting. The whole tree, uprooted trunk and massive branches, will endure even in death for many years. Another ax will be broken with each new attempt to cut a portion of it off; the smaller branches and limbs are long vanished.

As Rivadavia walks away from you afterwards in the direction of the pond, lost in the thoughts that you've given him, you sit alone in the silence, softly crying. Hidden in the tall grasses at water's edge, a chorus of toads and frogs is singing. In the water swims a solitary, white swan, craning its velvety neck to the sound of their song. Royal ducks with blue feathers, deep as lapis lazuli, and spotted geese with brilliant red beaks circle overhead, while a pair of iridescent flamingos step out of the water. Wiping bitter tears from your face, you sit erect and proud by the fire. You're remembering both sound and smell of your beloved Ranquel encampments. You feel your Indian husband's skin, caress your Indian children's faces.

Rivadavia, head bent downward thoughtfully as he walks toward the pond, soon collides with Mansilla whose glance is skyward, engaged by the honking of those magnificent birds. Later, calmed somewhat by his colonel's meditations on the confused nature of civilization and barbarism, he finds himself back at the campfire. A gourd of the green yerba maté is making its rounds; the meat is almost ready.

Mansilla laughs. He takes a sip from the gourd, presses his lips to the metal sucking-tube that filters the rough leaves of the maté tree from the mildly stimulant tea they produce. Sipping it, he sits back on the same dead trunk that Rivadavia has recently abandoned. He hands the gourd to him. The captain drinks and then passes it back to one of the soldiers. The soldier returns it to the fire where more water, not quite boiling, is added to the brew.

Another of the soldiers, mischievous and sly, whispers loudly enough for Mansilla to hear: "Maybe the colonel will tell us one of those tall tales of his."

"Yes!" comes the chorus of other voices. "Let's hear one of the colonel's stories!"

"Pay close attention," Mansilla says. "This is a good one to keep in mind when going through thick woods."

The circle grows tight around him, then, as he relates the jovial story of a certain muleteer and his adventures in the wild and woolly days of the provincial bosses, or caudillos. Chased into the mountains for his revolutionary associations, this muleteer winds up attached (by the locks of his long, tangled hair) to the branch of a locust tree. There, to keep from being found out, he plays dead. He spooks his pursuers by exclaiming long life to the local caudillo — in his best B-movie, horror-flick voice — just as they catch sight of his swinging corpse. But for all this trouble, he's reduced some days later to such powerful hunger that, still swinging there, he eats his own shirt and dies of indigestion.

"And thus the story ends," Mansilla says. A bit vainly, he smiles. The soldiers, overjoyed with the novel ending, cheer. He takes a bow.

Beside him by the tree, from where you haven't moved since the captain walked away from your words, you smile sadly. That melancholy expression contains both your joy and all of your life's solitude.

Lucio Mansilla, basking still in the glory of that evening's storytelling, glances further around that fire until his eyes meet yours. And now he's curious about you, Rivadavia's stubborn captive. He's curious about that girl who, according to the captain's telling, was seduced by barbarism's attractions into abandoning the civilizing touch of her Christian mother's hearth. The colonel grows thoughtful, quietly pondering whether your life is improved by this new captivity or harmed. He invites you to tell your story: the reasons for your resistance to this unwished-for redemption.

"Tell us, señorita, the story of your life."

"That would be señora, my colonel. I may be young — eighteen or nineteen, best I remember — but I'm a married woman. Didn't the good captain tell you? You're not redeemed if torn from the husband and the children that you love."

"So tell us, señora, how it happened that you were torn from one family and still found contentment within another."

"I'll do that," you say, "but don't interrupt too much whilst I'm telling it. Don't do like that captain over there, who only bosses and never listens. Let me tell you, colonel, if he's anyone's savior, he's sure not mine."

"Go ahead," Mansilla answers. "I promise I'll listen with respect."

At this he sits down on the ground, drawing his poncho more tightly around himself against the cold. He leans in closer to where you're sitting and willingly meets your eyes.

"Thanks," you say. "Maybe hearing me now, you'll make him set me free. I'll tell you how it was as best I remember, but it's been a long time since I thought of that other world. I never asked for this unhappy remembering."

Chapter 2

In which a pampean childhood is recalled

When I was born I was called Dorotea Bazán. I'd almost forgot that name, but I'm remembering everything now, even my parents who must have loved me in their way but were always fighting and scolding.

I guess I loved them, too. I guess I was happy, though not as deep happy as I'd come to be later with my Ranquels. My father, when he wasn't tipping the bottle, could be real affectionate, even funny. My mother was, in her way, a saint, always praying to her little Virgin and putting up with my father's anger that'd flare up at her whenever he was drunk. She only worked; I don't think she'd ever had time to play. When I wanted her to play with me, she'd only fuss and shoo me away from our little shack. I grew up outside with the other scabby children, and with the mangy dogs and other animals that roamed our streets. I had the run of the neighboring fields.

We lived in a little village on the border there with San Luis. It was all the world we knew.

I remember real clear-like that, with a certain boy, I'd run down to a creek, overhung with willows that we'd play under, and he'd tell me stories of Indians, frightful tales of raids and captives who got to be as savage as their captors. We'd run beneath those trees, anyhow, and I'd play the part of the helpless maiden in the grasp of a ruthless warrior. That horrid game haunted my dreams afterwards but I still couldn't resist, like some part of me already knew. Once, he tied my hands with a rope he'd stole from somewheres along our ramblings. Then — he might have been imitating his own *winca* father, or mine — he acted like he'd heard the lustful savage always would. He kissed me hard on the mouth, bit the lip. My first kiss. It hurt. Then he struck my mouth with the back of his hand. I wasn't more'n six years old, I think. He must have been eight or nine. Crying, lip bleeding, I ran and didn't stop till I'd reached our shack. When I got there, my father was inside beating on my mother. I loosed the rope from my own wrists by myself. I dried my own tears.

I don't remember much about the years right after that. I just know I didn't play with that boy no more. I don't remember his bothering me, neither. I wouldn't know if out of shame. But what I *can* tell you is what happened a few years later. When I must have been about ten. There was a real raid, and for some reason I can't explain, my parents and me weren't among those taken, though the father of a little girl who lived close by us was. The picture of her screaming, arms stretched out after him whilst he's snatched away by a swarm of warriors with their knives, is stuck here in my head as clear like it was happening right now. I don't even know if I really saw that. I don't know how I could have. It seems all imagined. But I do know that many times I heard her cry. She must have really loved that father. I don't remember him ever raising his voice against her or her mother, who for all I know might have been captured then, too. Somehow the child stayed behind. Who knows if anyone ever comforted her?

We weren't long at getting our revenge, though. I remember hearing where a band of our men went out against the Indians and killed a good dozen of women and children, unprotected by their men who were out hunting ostriches with their bolas. That much I was only told, but I saw what they did to the Indian child they brought back with them. I've never for a moment forgot the fear I saw in her eyes. It was like the fear I'd felt myself that time my pretend captor's play got violent and real. Only many times fiercer because she knew she wasn't ever going to escape. I sensed every bit of what she was feeling, how horrible it would have been. And I saw what some of them did to her without them knowing I was watching. When they left her, naked and bloody, she looked dead. I couldn't move from the spot, not to flee or approach to where she was laying. Night fell and I curled up into a trembling ball of loneliness, suffering from all the cruelty I'd ever known or ever would. When morning came, not even looking to see if she was still there, I ran home like some scared rabbit. I fell down crying on the bed where my mother was still stretched out from her own night's wrestle with my father. Her own unspoken sorrows.

Chapter 3

In which I make a transition

At this point you lapse into silence, my poor Dorotea-Leeza. You shiver, glancing up at the shimmering moon. A soldier, catching a look from his commander, Mansilla, approaches you with another poncho, which you take with a grateful nod and slip over your shoulders.

"Anyhow," you say, sighing for the part of your tale that you've found no words for, "I can't tell you no more of that childhood. Maybe it was better'n that. My parents happier, my time less violent. Like I said, it's been a long while and I can't be too sure of my memory."

Mansilla, already entranced by your legend, can only nod his head. "There are such mysteries in the human heart," he muses within himself, not speaking. "Abysses so deep in love, self-denial, and generosity that words will never explain them."

Rivadavia sits down beside Mansilla, captivated too (against his own will) by your words.

"Go ahead," Mansilla urges. "What happened then, after you'd grown up a bit more?"

"I'll tell you of starting to become a woman," you say, "and of my first love."

Chapter 4

Of a young woman's labors and a furtive romance

When I got to be about twelve years old, I started having a woman's monthly troubles. My mother said it was time I learned to work. She set me up as a servant in the judge's house, a spread so big it seemed ages before I could find my way around all of it without feeling lost.

I hadn't known there could be such splendor. At home, the three of us lived in a space not much bigger'n his servants' outhouse. I marveled at it and then felt sad. It troubled me that some had so much whilst the rest of us so little, or nothing at all. I wondered why that was so, if it'd always been that way. And I got to thinking it must have to do with why rich folks treat us poor ones so bad. So they could keep it that way, maybe, like there wasn't enough to go around. I only just assumed it must be everywheres like the way that judge and his pampered wife treated their servants.

First I had to learn to wash their clothes and the clothes of their lazy children who were older'n me. I learned to scrub their marble floors and clean the house from top to bottom. There were a million other daily chores it's not worth the trouble of remembering. And then, whenever it'd catch one of their fancies, they'd invent something so trivial like doing up the daughter's hair just right or sewing a button on the son's shirt, whilst I still had other work that if it wasn't done by nightfall I'd be punished.

The judge never punished me himself. I was too far below him. But if he gave the word — it was enough just to raise a brow and look back down at some paper or other — the missis would lay in all alone. If she didn't like something I'd done and wanted to make a point of it she'd grab me by the arm, press so hard it bruised, then haul me before him even if it meant traipsing clear across the grounds. If he was away, or she just wanted done with it faster, she'd slap me and punch me and even throw me to the floor. When I was down, one of those brats might go by and kick me real hard in the belly or groin, to where it's a wonder I could ever grow up to have *my* own children. Maybe I should have said something to my mother, but I think she must have known anyhow, if only for the marks on me that the missis never tried hiding. Besides, my mother had her own troubles. Maybe she was teaching me not to expect too much from life.

I think Missis Judge was taking it out on me cause of some unfaithfulness on the part of her husband. I heard her say something about it to her son when she'd got wind of the son running after some village girl or other. When she caught me listening to that, distracted for a second by unlucky curiosity, she hit me on the mouth with her clenched fist. I think that's why she abused me sometimes in front of her husband, too, cause she couldn't hit him for what she knew he was doing behind her back. She hit me in the mouth, anyhow, and that was all I could stand for one day. She broke one of my teeth that I spit out at her, all bloody, after I'd almost swallowed it. Right away, before she could do anything else, I ran off onto the plain and hid along the creek bed, where I slept that night in the tall grasses, downstream from the trees where I'd used to go with that boy. When I came back to work the next morning, nobody said nothing, and my mother didn't ask no questions when I came home the second night with swelled lips.

It was about that time, somewheres between twelve and thirteen, that I met my first love. He was older'n me, maybe eighteen, and he come on me once of an evening whilst I was sitting under a tree, nursing that day's tears by myself before drying them for the walk home.

He was a handsome boy, tall and rugged, and I loved him as soon as I'd met his eyes that seemed so unexpected soft for a man's. They caressed me like no other eyes before. Then he touched my face with those gentle fingers, rough from his day's labors yet noways harsh. Soon — I can only imagine how it happened — he was kissing me and I was letting him. He was holding me in his arms. After that he was making love to me whenever he could, but only so far as I'd let him. You understand I was still real young, scared by what I'd seen them do to that Indian girl before leaving her for dead. I wasn't sure I wouldn't end up dead, too. Sometimes I'd pull away from him with that thought hard in my head. But then he'd just smile and start talking. And his talking was the most beautiful noise I'd ever heard, more soothing than the babbling of that mountain stream that'd always be rolling on down beside us. I'd lie back then in the grass, just listening whilst he went on. His words were like dreams. The world he made with them was peaceful and calm. His words made me forget how alone I'd always felt, would always feel when daily living forced them out of my heart. But then, whenever I could get away, they'd come back to fill me. And there he'd be.

He was a hard-working boy, he had his troubles, too. There wasn't time or money for the rich people's schooling but he could read some. He'd always loved stories, so whenever some singer or other'd come around he'd gather up close and listen. He had those songs by heart. He'd gathered up a couple of books, too. He could read them far enough to guess at the parts he wasn't sure of. He'd tell me sometimes about men in far off lands who'd dress up for protection in clothes of some kind of metal, then go out defending poor folks like us against all the evil giants and dragons in the world. Those stories of his were the strangest. They were the ones I loved the most. I imagined he was the one in that metal suit. That nothing could hurt him as long as he wore it. And that I was safe, too, long as he was there protecting me. And you know? In the strangest way I believed all his words were real. The giant in his story was my judge and the dragon his wife who burned me with her evil breath. Only Alonsito understood and defended me. I'd stay with him late into the night, creep home when the sun was almost ready to come up. I'd fall asleep in the grass beside that water, dreaming of those magical tales. Then when I woke up I might see him sleeping, too. Leaning back against the tree but with his head slumped forward slightly over me. Like even then he was keeping watch. Against anyone who might try hurting me.

It was after one of those nights my father caught us. I'd fell asleep with my head on his lap whilst my sweet Alonso, my precious Alonsito, was caressing my face and hair with his gentle hands, like with his words he'd been caressing my heart. I woke up later than usual, whilst the sun's tip was barely making itself known. He was softly shaking me awake, whispering something that at first I didn't understand. He knew who my father was, cause they'd done some odd work together. Then I understood it was my father's name he'd whispered: Señor Bazán. My father was standing over us. I got up fast, fixed my dress so nothing was showing. I ran like the wind to my work and didn't look back.

When I went that night to the usual place, hoping for at least a brief word and a plan so I could go on seeing him, my father was there instead. He just looked at me for the longest time, like he'd forgot who I was and was trying to remember. I held up my head and looked back at him, but I didn't know what to say. Then he just started beating on me, for the first time ever that I can recall. I'd seen him hit my mother, but he'd never hit me. Whenever he was drunk like that I stayed well hid, but now he hadn't drunk nothing. He hit me, sober like I'd never seen him. He kicked me till I finally blacked out. I don't remember what happened after that, but I woke up at home on our only bed. My womanly troubles were on me again and I was bleeding fresh blood onto the filthy mattress. The blood on my face was crusty and hard. Even my mother hadn't bothered to clean it. Like I said, she had problems of her own.

Chapter 5

In which Mansilla contemplates the nature of love

At this point you once more fall silent. Your listeners at the fire, intent on what you've been telling, barely stir.

"A father like that should be horsewhipped himself," says Rivadavia, visibly altered by the tale. "See how he likes it."

Mansilla, pondering the terrible contrasts that exist within a single human heart, can't help but imagine the father's other suffering now, since losing his daughter perhaps forever.

"Do you know if he's still living?" he asks, jumping slightly ahead of the story.

"I'm not sure, colonel," you answer, "but I've heard from those coming back from raids now and then that my mother's been living with some other man for a while, and he was taken off in some military conscription or other. Or else he escaped into the mountains over by Chile."

When you finish talking, the audience that's gathered around that fire is engulfed in a melancholy silence that for a moment is only broken by the night sounds of La Verde, and then gradually by the hushed murmurings of soldiers who speak of characters they've known who are very much like the ones you're describing.

Mansilla, carried away by his wonder at the true, unadorned history that you've so far related, is pontificating silently to himself on the nature of human solitudes and love.

"And speaking of love," he soliloquizes, "say what the ruling classes will, it exists like its twin, happiness, only in life's extremes. Not in comfort, not in the sameness of ordinary, cultured life, but in whatever rips us away from the predictability of our normal, and usually hateful, routines.

"I can understand, for instance," he continues, "the love of any Romeo for his Juliet. I understand the hate of a man, Silva for his enemy Hernani, and I also understand the greatness of forgiveness. But I don't understand those sentiments that respond to nothing energetic or strong, to nothing terrible or tender."

You return to your story. You speak calmly but slowly, as if only in that manner you can contain the deep emotion that your memory is stirring in you. Mansilla, as you speak, is extracted by those words from his reveries.

Chapter 6

Of tragic romance and fated captivity

I don't know what they told the judge and his wife. But I didn't go back there to work for more'n a week. After that they wouldn't give me a chance to get near Alonso. When it was time for me to come home at night, one of them would be there to get me. I'd look out a window sometimes during the day and catch a glimpse of him off in the distance, looking back at me. But that was as close as he'd get to me for the longest time. I didn't know what my father'd done to him, or what he still might do, but I was hoping Alonso'd put on that metal suit, that he'd come and free me from the captivity I was trapped in. Then, almost like I'd hoped him into being, there he was beside me for one tiny moment whilst the missis and her brood weren't around. He was there for just a second, long enough to hint to me of a plan. There'd be horses. Or one, because I could ride with him. The first full moon, at the moment the little goats were at their highest point in the sky. He'd be waiting. Right away I'd be up and he'd sweep me away. He wouldn't let anyone else touch me without my leave.

From then till the appointed night, I knew I couldn't hide my happiness. So I tried to make them think I'd forgot about him, that I'd finally just come around to their way of thinking. When my mother came that first evening to take me home, I kept up a cheerful chatter the whole way. Then I hugged my father and asked him to forgive me.

I still didn't think he suspected nothing, and when I laid down to sleep that longed-for night in the open air outside our shack, under the perfectly round moon, I didn't give no sign of what I was planning. But my mother must have guessed something cause she was watching me funny. And when I rose up after they'd been sleeping inside for quite some time, whilst I got up from my bed under the starry sky, I thought I heard her stirring. I ran as fast as my legs would take me, faster'n before when I'd run from that boy, but not fast enough. Just as I'd got close enough to hear the horse's whinnying, to see my Alonsito slip out from behind his tree, I looked over my shoulder and saw my father coming.

He caught up to us just as I was up on the horse, just as Alonso was in motion to leap up behind me. My father lunged with his long-bladed knife and caught him beneath the arm. It must have gone clear through the heart, judging from all the blood that followed in torrents. My truest love fell back on the ground and was lost to me. My heart stopped beating with his.

It must have been right then, cause I can't remember another thing, that a Ranquel warrior swooped down on me. His torso glistened in the moonlit night, glistened in that light whilst my heart finished breaking. He snatched me up and carried me off on his horse. The last thing I remember is my father's voice, fading away whilst I looked back over my shoulder. I remember him calling out to me then — "Dorotea! Forgive me, daughter! I'm sorry, my child! Forgive me!"— like after what he'd done there was any chance of that.

Chapter 7

In which Rivadavia holds forth on bloodthirsty barbarism

And that's all you can say just then. It's as if the words themselves have sapped you of all remaining energy, and you slump down in a genuine swoon. It's one of the other captives, anxious herself to be reunited with her Christian babies that she's been separated from since their infancy, who comes to you at that moment and holds you. Soon, you would appear to be sleeping soundly, though in hardly a moment you'll sit up again and resume your narrative. For now, though, you rest, head on the lap that has so suddenly proffered itself. She runs her fingers through your hair and looks off into space, perhaps thinking of the many hardships of a woman's free moments as well as of her captivities. She smiles enigmatically. Sadly. A large bird swoops down past her head and lands on the edge of the water.

A second bird follows the first. Rivadavia, caught between divergent lines of thought on what his countrymen would generally dismiss as that "Indian problem," watches as it lands gracefully beside its partner. Looking from the birds to Mansilla, he releases a heavy sigh and shrugs his shoulders.

"I don't know," he says. "These Indians, whatever else you might say about them, are still savages. They have no true religion. What comfort can they offer a woman of our race?"

He can't shake the poet's image of their barbarous festival: warriors satiating themselves on blood as it flows hot from the mare they've just killed, sucking it like vampires as it falls from the freshly slashed throat.

"That's a scene I've witnessed often enough since I've been in Indian country," he says. "You've witnessed it too, Colonel. You described a similar spectacle to me just the other day. The gift mare that was demanded of you? Your eventual consent? Caniupán and his braves lapping its blood from the ground before stripping its bones, like starved dogs, of their last traces of meat?"

Mansilla, sipping long and hard at the yerba maté, listens for the moment without responding. He's reflecting on other, contradictory images that his friend, though struggling against them, is not unaware of.

Indeed, Rivadavia is frustrated by the stubborn reality of your complaint, which contrasts so deeply with the idealized role that he's expected you to play. He's still bracing himself against those paradoxes. He's appealing for comfort to the inflexible dramatizations of that narrative poem that he's heard recited, whose heroine acts precisely as she should. And whose Indians, baldly stereotyped as the purest forces of evil, behave like so many demons escaped from some remote corner of Dante's Hell.

Do you know the story, Leeza? Argentina's first Romantic poet, Echeverría's *The Captive*? It goes like this. The noble Captain Brian and his valiant wife María are swallowed up by the immeasurable wilderness that stretches out open and mysterious at the feet of the Andes. But not before she steals bravely, with "manly" strength, from the drunken camp where she's only momentarily captive. She escapes, a lone woman, from her captors' lair, bludgeoning a stirring savage before he can sound the alarm. Then she rescues her husband who's staked out to die on the pampa, bound by tight ropes and arms open beside him to form a cross. She coaxes him further into those empty spaces, singlehandedly fights off some pampean cat looking for easy prey. Only when his wounds are too much for him and he finally dies does her end loom also. She's found at last on that vast pampa by Brian's soldiers. But when she asks about her son, some "unholy" voice tells her that he's dead, his throat slit by those heathens. And upon hearing that crude report (never mind that until now she's been Amazonian in her feats of strength) she falls down like a dry stalk that, at the slightest gust of wind, breaks in two. The courageous soldiers cry for her and give her a funeral that's truly worthy of such sublimely noble womanhood.

Meanwhile, back at the ranch, as they say, while the infidel tribe still slept, a terrible vengeance was being prepared for it. Soon, as dawn was just breaking, the confused cries of Indian women and children were heard on those plains.

"Foreigner surrounding us, Christian traitor," they called.

And the Christians made a horrible, horrible killing that day, neither woman nor man nor child of that tribe remaining against the unstoppable slaughter. Those redeemed captives shed tears of joy at their liberation, but they were sad when no trace of Brian was found anywhere (until, as already related, much later, tragically later).

Get a load of this, Leeza! What baloney! These Indians of the poet's fantasy hardly receive a single sympathetic glance from him. The poet himself had never set foot in this vast backcountry. He wouldn't have known an Indian if one bit him in the ass. Only at better than a century later do most readers begin to feel with a stabbing sense of remorse, from something like the Indians' perspective, this poignant scene of women and children unfeelingly slaughtered. The poet and his average contemporary just see the Indians' inevitable and mindless debauchery. The soldiers' vengeance is the poet's prophecy of civilization's rightful triumph. The Indian only exists as an obstacle in the way of Argentina's own manifest destiny.

Rivadavia, anyway, is confused by Mansilla's silence, which echoes resting Dorotea's. He's swallowed up in his solitary imagining of that fabled captain and his noble wife, whose magnificent courage and terrible solitudes were undoubtedly big enough to fill the whole South American continent.

One of the former captives, angry at the violence of her particular captivity, joins this complaint to her redeemer's: "Curse them all, those savages! And that little whore who's so hot to stay with them, too."

And one of the soldiers:

"God knows we've all suffered at their hands. Who hasn't known someone, family or neighbor, snatched away while the Indians with their fire don't leave a single house standing?"

"And yet," says Mansilla's interpreter Mora, a half-breed from one of the Ranquel villages, "the Indians have suffered, too, at the Christians' hands. They aren't any more unfeeling or cruel than the average human being."

"And I also seem to remember," Mansilla adds, "other scenes from my own recent excursion to these Ranquel Indians. Such as the women in Baigorrita's camp who, far from savaging the mare while its life slowly expires, first knock it cold with a compassionate blow to the head."

To himself, remembering the remarkable sense of unselfconscious egalitarianism that the Indians share among themselves: "These barbarians have established the law of the Gospel — today for you, tomorrow for me — without falling prey to socialism's utopias. Of course, this is opposite of what happens among Christians, where if a man doesn't have means, he doesn't eat."

Meanwhile, dear Leeza-Dorotea, you're beginning to shake off the last vestiges of that weariness that had briefly overcome you. In a moment you'll be ready to continue your truthful narrative.

Chapter 8

On the none-so-gentle attentions of Ranquel and other women

I can't remember that Ranquel warrior's figure. At least not really remember, cause at that point, my remembering seems more like some kind of dreaming. It's like when Alonso fell back dead, I died with him and started dreaming this other life. And the dreaming itself started fixing the memories of that other life onto it. That life that, for all I knew, I might have just imagined. When I saw that warrior's face, then, I was putting my Alonsito's face onto it. So I let him carry me away without resisting. I've got no idea how long it was before I woke up, but it must have happened to the feeling of being kicked. Just in case I'd get the idea that things would be easy here.

I can't remember if I ever saw that Indian again. When I woke up, I was in a different man's tent. At least it seemed to be someone else's, though how could I really know? But this man, it seemed to me, was older'n the young warrior of my dream, and he was a captain over some twenty or thirty men. He never treated me like his woman, or forced any other violence on me, but he didn't defend me from anything neither. And in those early times there was more'n enough violence being forced on me by the other women.

First there were his wives. He had three of them, one who seemed more important than the others. He'd shed his favors from time to time on the other two, but she was the one he clung to most regular and who'd sleep in the place of honor every night. He'd get up whenever it caught his fancy and visit one of the other wives, then return to that place where he'd start snoring beside wife number one, who'd pretend she hadn't noticed nothing and be no more'n a little colder to the other in the morning. More often than not it was number one he was making love to, and no doubt she had some prestige over the others, cause they always did her bidding. The first wife just gave me work and left most of the meanness to the other two. They were worst on mornings after they'd felt real neglected.

One night not long after I'd come there, he was all naked, crawling to the other who was waiting. I felt his hot gaze and looked up to see him watching me. He'd stopped there for a moment like to size me up, to see if he wanted to try me out. I met that gaze coldly, then turned quick away. I was afraid of taking in the rest of his body. I hid my face and prayed silent-like he'd go away. Then I realized he already had. I don't know what he saw to make him respect me like that, or if he didn't just think I was ugly. But maybe it was how young I was. I could have been his granddaughter. Or that I hadn't showed him no fear. Whatever. He left me alone after that, never gave me no kind of trouble. But I still got a good enough beating for it, from the wife he visited then. Also a kick from the first one and a bigger beating from the other, who hadn't even got a glance.

But my worst trouble came from the other captives, whilst I would have thought, of all people, they'd be my friends. It must be true what people say, that a blow feels better when you pass it on. Maybe that's how it was with my father, who took out all his troubles by beating my mother. And me, too, when it struck him I might try breaking away. I guess that could be any of us if we don't make a conscious choice to be different. I made that choice, myself. If I ever got out from under those women's lashings, I'd never turn my strength on someone I could help. No need making myself vile like them.

Those fellow captives — there were two besides me — hardly gave me a moment's peace from when I got there to when I left. And that really got their goat when I did go. Maybe it was to keep that from happening, they were so rough. Like by keeping me covered in grime and bruises, no warrior'd ever look at me and snatch me away instead of them. Or maybe in some part of their heads they wanted to protect me against giving in to that savage lust. Some captives would sooner die than give in to it. But some were only wanting a warrior for themselves, I think. Even though in that case their troubles might only get worse. Long as an Indian's coming around nights to visit some captive, come day, she'll get bad treatment from the women she lives with. Just soon as he stops bothering about her, they'll leave her alone again. Even if he does take her off, she'll almost never be his main wife, so there's always someone who might look down on her.

I remember one of those earliest days. It'd just rained, and they dragged me down to the creek that ran past our village and made me wash clothes. Then they ganged up on me whilst the wives stood back and watched. They tore my dress and beat me till my skin was bleeding all over. They pushed me into the mud and threw the clothes I'd just washed in on me. They pushed me down some more, all the while never letting up with the kicks and punches. I laid there curled up like I was still in my mother's belly. I had to fight not to cry out loud. Then they shouted I'd let the clothes get dirty again, better get up and get them washed. When I did, they joined those wives and laughed. I just kept my face turned away from them. When I tried to use the water to wash myself, to wash the clothes I wore that were filthy with mud, they yelled and chased me back to our tent. I collapsed there in a heap. I slept there till the next morning, when I knew it'd start all over again.

Chapter 9

Of labors, liberties, and a warrior's protection

My daily labors were to wash and cook and tend to the horses, look after the babies, haul water, and haul wood for the fires, do anything at all that might catch anyone's fancy. Cause I didn't belong to just one man, but to all his women and their Christian slaves, too. Also to any Ranquel visitor who might pass by and ask me to do something no one else'd thought of.

I was really a slave. But I'd already got a notion of some freedoms, too. Sometimes, when left alone, I'd almost dance through those wild spaces. Some part of me'd already took a liking to them. I'd smell those raw smells and feel almost at home. It felt like something I'd been missing in that other world, and anyhow I wasn't going back there. I was happiest when sitting at some neighboring fire — we were pretty well free to roam, long as no one didn't come looking — sitting there with the little children who'd teach me words in their language. More important, they taught me there could be real tenderness in that world. I'd catch the briefest look some mother'd give her girl, or a father the boy he hoped would grow up to be a proud warrior. I knew this was a place I might come to feel safe in, if only I could find a way to show them all that I belonged there. That I didn't want to go back.

First time I ventured out into the countryside away from the village, I knew right away I was being followed. Like they wanted to stop me if I tried escaping. But I didn't even want to escape. There wasn't no single other place I could think of going to. The boy I'd loved was dead, killed by my own father. I couldn't forgive him or ever come near him. As for my mother, well, what do you think? She'd been careful about remembering me in her little prayers to the Virgin, but she'd never done nothing to defend me in the flesh. I'd seen more tenderness already between an Indian woman and her child, who was let to run free and learn to work at her mother's side. Like the boy learned an Indian's labors just as matter-of-fact at his father's side. Or at some other warrior's, if his father was dead. No one sent those children to be mistreated by some powerful chief or his wife, like I was sent to that judge's house. Out there, no Indian was any better than another. Only the captives had to suffer everyone's abuses. The Indian women suffered, too, but not like the captives, who'd always get the worst of it if they couldn't make themselves fit in.

I came out onto that plain, anyhow. I knew I was being followed. But I pretended not to notice, tried making an impression on them. I looked up at the sky, big like the pampas; I couldn't tell where one started and the other stopped. And I just threw back my head, let out the biggest savage yelp my voice could muster. My eyes were closed and I spun myself around in a circle. I fell down on those grasses and laughed. Exploded with what I could, then, of the Ranquel language. Let them hear as plain as I could that I loved those lonesome spaces, that if I could help it I'd never be leaving them. When I knew they were gone I just laid there, soaked in all that silence. I only wandered back when the sun was already set. I was smiling like a cat in a chicken coop. Those women hardly knew what to make of me, they just left me alone for the rest of that evening. The Indian women maybe respected me a little more, but the other captives didn't know what to think. They laid in on me, all the same, after they'd had a little time to stew on it.

My life just kept on being hard with those women, but the beatings finally let up. What I didn't know was there could be even worse trouble than that. But while I was wandering, it'd been gathering. The younger warriors — boys just about my own age or a little older — started following me when I got away from the tents. Before long they were trying to have their way with me. The first couple of times I quick and escaped, but once not by much. I only got loose of him after I'd left the shape of my hand, red like the setting sun, plastered like a brand on that proud face. And then after I'd sunk my teeth into his arm.

I should interrupt now to tell you what freedoms the unmarried Indian girls have in those matters. Fact is, a warrior can come at night into any girl's tent, enjoy as much of her as she's willing to be giving, never worrying if mother or father hear him. If she turns him away he's got no choice but to leave. But no one'll look down on her if she consents. In that way she's freer than the married women, whose love isn't never for loan. And anyhow, once the Indians marry, they're much more faithful than Christians, both the men and the women. It may be an Indian's got more'n one wife, but only if he's rich enough in horses and other bounty that he'll still share all around. And he might be tempted by some captive woman he's got around the house. She's his property, after all. But you won't find him playing around with no other Indian's wife, just like you won't catch her with another man. If he suspects her of it, if he's a real drunk or ruthless sort, he might just kill her, but that kind of thing doesn't happen like on Christian soil, where I hear it's a regular event. I even bet when it does happen it's more cause of what's rubbed off of so-called Christian ways than the Indian's own native instinct. That's my opinion, anyhow. Given what I've been able to figure out on the subject.

But that's the way it goes for the Indian woman who's not married. Though she's not as free to say yes or no if a warrior asks to marry her. If he wants to, he's got three choices. Either to marry by love with the girl's consent, by force with the parents' help, or to just plain steal her. Anyhow, the Indian's got to pay something to the girl's family, but more in the last two cases. If he marries for love, he's out of luck if the girl changes her mind and goes back to her parents. But otherwise, she'll always be forced to return to him.

The captive woman has it harder. A marriage payment might still be made to the warrior who owns her, but in most cases she's not so lucky. Anyhow, whatever stories you might have heard, that boy by the river of my childhood didn't have it right about lustful Indians. They might look at a woman just like any man, but they usually don't go around raping them. Not even the captives.

There *was* that one boy, though. I was down by the creek washing clothes one morning when he came up behind me with a couple of friends. I couldn't even let out a cry, he put his hand on my mouth and pulled me down. His friends helped him hold me there whilst he tore at my dress. Both of my shoulders were exposed, he pawed my breasts. Him and his friends laughed. Then he pressed his knee into my groin. I think he would've finished raping me, maybe even let the others go at me afterwards, but just then my guardian angel saved me. When he'd freed me of them, that gentle warrior turned away, let me get covered. By his silence, I knew I could count on his further protections. In return, I reached out to him. I touched his face before I turned back to my washing. I wanted him to know I was thankful.

Chapter 10

An unwillingly redeemed captive speaks of names and identity

His name was soft like the hand that'd caught me up from my murderous father. Strong like that, too, perfect like the name he finally gave me. I already had one from the others, but his fit me better, his I kept. And then, soon as he whispered it to me, I really started forgetting my *winca* name, that old identity I'd no more need for. I'd have maybe *finished* forgetting it, if this captain hadn't tore me away again, thinking he was doing me some favor by forcing me where I couldn't never fit back in.

My husband's was a name I won't speak in this unfriendly place, made that way by the violence you great civilizers are doing me in it. I won't speak my name, neither. Let them stay unheard to you, like the lives you're tearing apart. You want to civilize this great pampa when you can't even understand it. And how can you understand it when you're only staring at the water in love with your own reflection? You don't even know your own people, the messes you've made of their lives, cast out in the desert like they are, with nothing, only your so-called civilization's scraps. Till you're one with this land, you can't bear to hear our real names. Even if you did, you wouldn't feel them. So as long as I'm here talking to you, I'll just be Dorotea, a girl of used-to-be. My husband and children, the ones our Great Father gave me and you're taking away, they're no part of you.

Anyhow, that husband of mine came back. He offered a full ransom to the captain who owned me. Not that he was rich; he didn't have hardly nothing. But to win my freedom, he'd gone on some raid and come back with a bunch of pretty little horses, fast as the wind they came on. He gave them all to that captain for me. And he didn't do it for lust, like maybe you think. He liked me good enough, I'm not saying he didn't want me. But if he did, he respected me more. He faced me to all the four winds and told me to go ever which way my heart'd take me. He loved me by that act, and because of it I loved him, too. It was to his tent that my heart made me follow. He'd turned away soon as he said those words, refused to look back. I don't know if he heard me following, but I went straight to his tent. It was a ways off from the others, separate. It was there he made me his wife.

There was no ceremony except this. He turned to face me, smiled and took both my hands. He caressed my hair, held me tight to his chest, slid the dress from my shoulders and let it fall at my feet. He took me to his bed. He was naked too, but that night he only held me. That's what finished making that marriage holy for me, that he only held me. He could have done whatever he wanted with me, but he let me know I still had my freedom. I was still young, still afraid of those old visions, but he'd give me all the time I needed. He wasn't in no hurry; that's why his touch always felt so gentle to me. When I was ready after those first few days, he knew it was what I really wanted. He kissed my mouth then for the first time.

You're embarrassed, maybe, for a woman to talk so plainly to you about these things? But I want you to understand, no question about it. These Indians aren't all as savage like you think, and they might be your betters in loving. What's sure is I've loved this husband, and there's no doubt he's loved me too. We've had four little children together, and if you'll let me, I still want to give him more. We both love those children and they love us. We're all they've had, and now you've stole me away.

We're not religious the way you'd have us be, we don't have no churches or worship no little saints. But we know there's a God. We call Him Cuchauentrú. He's the Great Man, the Great Father of us all. We worship Him without cult. He takes on human form and is everywhere, unseen and undivided. He only does good to His human children who can't help but love Him. But we also believe in a devil. We call him Walicho. He's got no form, but if he did, he'd look something like you. He's the one who causes the failed raids that our warriors die in. He's always going about the land, just like you, trying to see what new mischief he can cause us. He's real ambitious and likes to have his hand into everything that isn't even his. To keep him from harming us, we always give him the first bit of anything we eat or drink. Just like to keep you from swallowing us up, we say nice words when we can and move a little further out of your way so we can go on living in peace, even if it's only for a while longer.

We know, since you're more powerful than us, you won't let us play this game forever, but for now what else can we do? These are our lands, these my people. I want to be free to stay with them till there's no more future for us nowhere. I want to stay with them even then, to share whatever fate you have in store for them. That's all I want, all I'll ever ask you for.

Chapter 11

In which I indulge in a philosophical aside

"Living among savages," our loquacious colonel will later write in his *Excursion*, "I have recently come to understand why it's always easier to move from civilization to barbarism than from barbarism to civilization." And also: "There is no doubt that civilization has its advantages over barbarism, just not as many as those who say we're civilized claim for it."

From there, he'll launch into an ironic enumeration of that civilization's fruits, which he'll say consists of there being, among other things, an immense number of doctors, sick people, lawyers, lawsuits, rich people, poor people, lying periodicals, and dreadful, expensive hotels. He'll tell then of a specific hotel he once slept in whose beds contained all of the crawling vermin that God — "in His infinite and primitive backwardness, thinking that they were good" — had created on the fifth day. He'll slip at last from that anecdote's supple thread into a bemused reverie about governments' generally unmet responsibility of guarding their people against various evils, from poor hygiene to perpetual warfare.

"Certainly," he'll say to wrap up that wandering thought, "civilization is, of all the modern inventions, one of the most useful for the well-being and progress of man. But as long as government doesn't do anything about certain evils I'll continue believing, in the name of my scant experience, that you'll sleep better on the street or on the pampa than in some hotels."

Chapter 12

And another aside

This, dear Leeza, from Mansilla's pen on the subject of Dorotea's accusation against his conquering race: "There's no greater evil than civilization without mercy."

The year of writing? Of his Ranquel excursion and this previously undiscovered encounter? 1870. Within approximately the next decade, as the United States is approaching the conclusion of its own Indian wars, this parallel extermination on Argentina's pampas will be effectively complete.

Chapter 13

In which the smallpox comes and Dorotea meets it

Our children were born two at a time, about three years apart from each other. Then came the smallpox that almost killed them and my husband both. That was an agony I thought'd never leave us.

It started after your leaders'd sent some new cargo of gifts. In the hands of that priest Burela who always brings so much liquor that the men around Mariano Rosas's tent, or around Baigorrita's or Ramón's, almost never stop their wild drinking. Then the ones that gave it turn around and act so disapproving, like they expect us to wash in it. He also brought other things, like some blankets I think might have deliberately carried the pox. At least I heard those first houses that got the sickness had new blankets in them. I saw them myself in one house. I'd gone to take care of the sick women and children abandoned there. The families were all terrified. They were taking off running into the spaces 'round about till the sickness'd pass.

You don't have to ask why the Indians are scared of that sickness. It kills them like ants in a fire. They never knew it till the Christians came. They thought it was a curse from heaven for some sins they'd committed, drawing near to that *winca* devil. They wouldn't go near the sick people, even the most loved wife or child, parent or brother or sister. They'd only leave food and water for as many days as they could, hoping it'd at least keep them over till they died. Otherwise there wasn't nothing more they could force themselves to do. The only way to comfort them in their pain was to go out raiding and killing. It was the only way they knew to let go of some little bit of their rage.

Sometimes that fear and rage'd make them do terrible things. Like they killed the blue-eyed captive boy they blamed for the sorcery that was spreading the sickness. I was an Indian now, my children half Indian by blood. But I didn't feel safe from such a thing happening to me, too. I had to do something to save myself. But more'n that, I had to do it out of love for my husband's people. Out of love and forgiveness, for whatever wrong'd been done to me. What happened to them was what happened to me. I wasn't just *me* no more; I felt like I was part of *them*.

I remember like it was yesterday, going into that first tent. I remember the clamminess of their poisoned skin whilst I lifted each of their heads to let them sip some water. Everything about that place tasted like sneaking death. I didn't know what to do. I visited some more places, found the same thing everywhere. Finally, I thought to get them outside into the cool air at some remove from the stricken tents that the survivors'd later burn. I almost ran, then, from tent to tent. Dragged them out by myself. Took hold of them from behind, under their arms, let their feet slide along the ground. When I couldn't go no further, I'd just fall back myself, let the diseased body of the one I was carrying fall right down on top of me. Soon as I'd caught my breath, I'd rise up again and start over, keep on dragging. When I got everyone settled, I'd bring new rounds of water with the few bits of meat I could get them to swallow in some broth.

Then, mostly, I just kept vigil on them, giving them what nourishment I could, snatching what bits of rest I was able while keeping a fire going inside the ring of their fevered bodies. Couldn't put them back in some old diseased tent, nor in another one that'd just get diseased itself. So I kept vigil. I massaged their cold limbs to give them warmth. I covered what I could of their bodies with bits of rawhide and worn old blankets. Then I'd fall asleep, jerk my head up again to tend the fire that was going out, make my rounds again to care for those poor suffering souls.

Amidst all that labor I must've dragged my own body home a couple of times, to hug my children and cry to my husband, rest my head against his chest. Because when I'd been at it for some days, I found my own family sick. I blamed myself for bringing it home to them. I wasn't sick myself, but I hurt so bad I ran out onto the pampa and just screamed. If I lost them, I'd have nothing left at all; I might as well die, too. I was so blinded by fear, I thought about taking my own knife right there and ending all our torment for good. But I pulled myself together and started doing the same thing for them I'd been doing for the others. When I'd carried my babies outside, then dragged my husband after, I took care of them with every loving gesture I could think of. Then I remembered the others and had to check on them.

It was like the whole village was only me and the dying or dead, cause some of them'd already escaped my care. I didn't know what else to do. What I decided was just pull the dead into some tent where the plague'd been that was closest by. I kept the living in that one central place. With them, soon as I could manage it, I put my own husband and children. At night after that, like before, I kept a fire going all night against the chill. I slept what I could, right there on the ground with them. I'd be praying all the while that they'd live.

Well, they didn't all, but once a few more had died, some of the others did start coming around. My husband and the children, too. Myself, I'd held out just long enough to see them coming back. Then I fell over sick with the very same fever. I don't remember nothing for a long time after that, just one evening I woke up and my husband was looking down at me. My head was resting on his lap whilst he kept wiping my brow with some wet cloth. When I sat up, I saw the old tents'd all been burned with everything in them. New ones were just going up and we'd come in there to stay closer to the others. The children were running and playing; they'd been cared for by various women I'd helped Cuchauentrú bring back from death's border. When they saw me well, they ran up and kissed me. I slept peaceful again that night. I didn't move my head from my husband's breast. The children huddled up against us both.

Chapter 14

Of Civilization's Faux Triumph over Barbarism

After relating this story, Dorotea takes a long sip from the maté gourd that has just then reached her. As she sucks that green liquid slowly through the *bombilla*, her eyes rest on Mansilla, who has seemed especially rapt as she spoke of that ordeal to save her adopted people.

"Please accept my sincerest admiration, señora, for that tremendous labor," the good colonel says. "I doubt that many of my men — or even I — could do alone what only Cuchauntrú, as you say, helped you to do."

As the soldier adds more water to the maté, my dear Leeza-Dorotea, you nod and give Mansilla only the most wan of smiles. But he doesn't need much encouragement.

"And I do know something of that terrible pox, too," he says. "You have just reminded me of my friend Chief Ramón's younger brother, Linconao. Ramón sent him to me, at my headquarters at Río Cuarto, as a sign of friendship."

He's a vigorous young man of twenty-two years and many excellent qualities, Mansilla says, launching straight into the story of how he saved Linconao from that same outbreak. Hauled him out of that tent — he'd been set up along with the other Indians outside the fort, alongside a little creek that runs into the Cuarto River — almost single-handedly, to hear the colonel tell it. With only a slight assist from the soldier attending him, he carried him out to the waiting cart, after delivering some weak words of encouragement to his fellow sufferers. The other Indians, keeping a wide distance from their sick companions, wouldn't dare lend a hand.

"That was a true victory of civilization over barbarism, of Christianity over idolatry," Mansilla would later write in his *Excursion*. Though in present company he is scarcely tempted to such a faux pas. Globetrotter and master orator that he is — and despite the occasional fit of pique (which maybe he's not above resorting to as political stratagem) — he is ever attentive to audience.

You respond, Leeza-Dorotea, with a slight quaver in your voice.

"Linconao is sure fortunate, Colonel, to have someone as bold as you looking out for him."

By way of counter-response, he offers the slightest but most gracious bow; while you continue wondering about those other poor Indians who lack such important fathers as Colonel Mansilla and Chief Ramón.

"And now, with your leave, my Colonel, I come to matters that touch more directly on you. That recent frontier diplomacy of yours."

"Once again you have my full attention, señora," he says with a flourish and a smile. "And however your judgments might occasionally pierce me, I'll try to keep my peace."

Chapter 15

Of Ranquel preparations for Mansilla's heroic excursion

"It wasn't too long after, word started reaching our villages of more *wincas* on their way to visit us. That's you, Colonel Mansilla, with those few men we see with you now around this fire. Come to bargain the terms of your country's peace.

That's what the messengers you'd sent ahead told us you were up to. Whether it was a peace that'd be any good to our country, to our Ranquel people in their lonely pampas, that was harder to say. And there were bound to be suspicions of who might be coming after. It was even questioned if you were really who you said you were.

Any man who'd ever been at the frontier since you'd been there would speak good of you, Colonel. They'd say you were a man of your word. That you'd treated the Indians visiting you there with a mix of truthfulness, impatience, and grouchiness, depending on the mood they found you in. But you weren't an Indian; we couldn't be sure you'd always keep to our best interests. There were lots of fears about what you maybe weren't saying, so you understand why we needed to prove there wasn't no trick coming up behind you before letting you come all the way into Leubucó. Into the very heart of Ranquel civilization. Into our main chief Mariano's village.

Mariano Rosas'd once been captive among the Christians. He knew them well. Maybe he did or maybe he didn't trust what you'd said you were up to. I met him once when he came to our village and I saw he was both warm and distrustful, even with his own people. We couldn't never be sure if he was believing in what we said. But we could tell he wasn't no fool, that he had his reasons for whatever he did. Aside from that, he's a man like any other. About forty-five years old, maybe. Long, thick hair that must have once been black like the night, and now's white like snow. His eyes are big and blue; they seem filled with both energy and a terrible sadness. They show him wild and proud. Protective of his Indian people.

Like I said, he was captive for some years whilst still a young man. He'd gone with his father, the famous chief Painé. They were on a raid somewheres around Buenos Aires, still out in the country a ways. He was staying back with some other boys to watch a group of horses that'd been kept there while their fathers went closer into enemy country. He was captured there and spent several years, servant to some big *winca* chief named Rosas. It's from him he got his name; before that, he'd been Painé like his father. Then, like he tells it, after he'd worked some years for this second father, him and the other captives all wanted to be free. They waited for a moonlit night and he led them all off on some of their captor's own horses. They wandered through the pampas till he'd finally found their way home. There, cause his Indian father'd just died, he inherited the whole kingdom. Later, the *winca* Rosas made a gift of mares, cows, bulls, sheep, also lots of life's other good things like yerba maté, sugar, tobacco. He invited the new Ranquel chief — he called him his godson — to visit him at the ranch, at his estancia in Buenos Aires province. But like I said, Mariano Rosas wasn't no fool. He read the invitation with lots of caution. He wouldn't never leave these places again. No way was he going to tempt fate a second time.

If Mariano Rosas had his reasons for distrusting, imagine those others' terror. The ones who'd never seen a Christian who wasn't captive. Who only knew what they heard or in their darkest imaginations invented. I saw how it was in our village, and later heard how it wasn't much different in Leubucó. Everyone here knows how you were made to wait there, Colonel, within a stone's throw of the Indians' tents, whilst you and your men were studied up and down by whoever wanted a look to see what could be read in your faces. Soon as those chiefs and captains and other Indians sent back their reports, the old diviners and seers'd study the signs. They would read the future and try to stop any evil fortune it might show. They would do all they could to ward off any of Walicho's presence, any harm that might be coming with these strangers.

My husband was one of the scouts sent to check the roads for any troops that might have been coming unannounced. Later, when they reported, it was like you'd said, that you really were Mansilla and no other troops were following you. So you were let into Leubucó even though some of the diviners'd only seen an evil fortune in your visit. Still, you were let in. Greeted with lots of ceremonies and drinking, like always when people visit in Ranquel territory.

By this time, if not from the beginning, Mariano Rosas must have already made up his mind. Maybe he sent back word to those prophets. Told them to look again till they got a different vision. Maybe they did, maybe they saw that nothing real evil'd happen whilst you were still there. But the future's another matter. Maybe Mariano knew the evil'd come anyway, with or without this visit. Maybe he was just bowing to what had to be, thinking he'd at least delay it a little, whilst getting all he could to relieve his people's poverty.

Now you say the Christians have done and'll keep on doing all they can to help the Indians. That's what my husband says of how you were talking in that big meeting. But I don't believe it, I'm thinking like Mariano Rosas. And this is what he said to you, Colonel, what my husband overheard in their more private talk, from some shadows where he was hid. "Brother," he said, "when the Christians have been able to, they've killed us, and if they can kill us all tomorrow they will. They've taught us to use fine ponchos, to drink maté, to smoke, to eat sugar, to drink wine, to wear riding boots. But they haven't taught us either how to work these fields the way they want them worked or brought us to know their God. So what services do we owe them then, brother?"

Chapter 16

In which Dorotea is wrenched from husband and children

I could never have guessed, when my husband got back from that meeting, that our time together was almost over. If I'd known, I'd have made the moment last forever. I'd have drowned all my loneliness in his strong embrace. I'd have held our children to my heart. We'd have let them fall asleep there beside us no sooner'n they wanted. Then him and me'd have stayed there holding each other the rest of the night, till in the morning they'd wake up. We'd never once close our eyes to our rawest feelings, to that physical love whose memory would help keep us alive while we're apart.

Or else we'd have took off the second we were warned, run into the vast pampas till you were gone. That would have been better, since you'd have never found us out, it would have saved us from this terrible separation.

Or when you showed up, captain, my husband could have stopped it himself, but you presented yourself by surprise with all your show of arms, a soldier right or left to back you up. Like you knew all along it wasn't the redemption you wanted everyone thinking it was. Just a new enslavement you'd have to back up with your civilization's ugliest force. He might have challenged you there, anyhow, caused more killing of our people then or later. But he'd never do nothing I didn't want, and with my eyes I told him to hold back. Nothing would be served answering your force with ours. My freedom would have to wait till Cuchauentrú wills it.

So that's how it was. And being unwarned, we couldn't have known nothing about it till it finally happened.

Anyhow, whilst my husband was coming up to our tent from the long journey home, I ran to him and hugged him. Kissed his cheek, invited him into our tent where I gave him something to eat and drink. He told me what he had to tell about that meeting. He seemed sad at the trouble he knew was coming on up ahead, cause he knew our people's days were numbered. He hugged our babies and kissed them good night, then laid down to sleep whilst I tucked them in next to us. It wasn't long till he was snoring. Then I laid down too, hugged him from behind, rested my head against his shoulder.

In the morning, we were barely out of our night's slumber when you surprised us, good captain. You were so dutiful and bold. You shouted that old name I'd almost forgot, the only one you and your colonel know me by. Then you said you'd come to save me from my long captivity. You said I was free to come since he'd let no one stop me. Then you had those soldiers point their weapons at my husband's neck, like he was the one forcing me and not you. Our children started howling. They couldn't understand a word of your Spanish, but they knew something evil was breaking up their happiness. They clutched my legs and held on. I was still stunned, only real slow understanding words that even to me sounded foreign and unreal. I threw my arms around my husband's waist. I pressed my face into that strong place between his shoulders, my breasts tight against his back. It was then you stepped forward yourself and gripped my arm. Tore me from those that love me and that I love. Forced me along a path I'd never have chose to walk.

You'll never erase my children's cry that went up to heaven, that cry that was still going up long after, whilst I was looking back at them, helpless myself, crying. You had to have noticed, but you still made me walk away from those babies, even whilst they were chasing after me and shrieking. Your heart must have been made stone right then, since you didn't even turn to look back. And I was crying loud as they were, cause my heart just wouldn't stop breaking. Then, when I was too far off to make out their individual faces, I could see the shape of them in their father's arms. The wide arms of that father who'd been struggling not to cry himself, otherwise he'd have grabbed them up sooner. His pain was all drawn inside of him so we'd only feel his strength, but in my heart I felt his tears and knew they hurt. His tears comfort me. Not cause of the pain he suffers but the love he feels. Cause he won't have forgot me. Cause whilst I'm gone our babies'll be safe like I was in those arms.

Chapter 17

In which I improvise what undoubtedly must follow

A gentle fog rises off of the pond and obscures the yellow moon.

Rivadavia, offended by such an uncomplimentary depiction of him, braces up his shoulders and launches into a speech to counter it. While you, Leeza-Dorotea, fall into another of your brooding silences.

"I'm as compassionate a man as any other you could name," Rivadavia says. "And I resent the treatment I've just had from a woman I've only done good to. When she was telling of the abuses she'd suffered as a little girl, didn't I murmur that someone other than herself should have taken the horsewhipping? And you can believe me when I say it tore me apart to hear those infants wailing. But I had no authority to free them with her, and even though it hurts her to leave them, surely someday she'll see this was best. Besides, if I'd have looked back like she suggests a feeling man would, I'd have broke down crying, too, and then how would I be honored and obeyed by those men I had following my orders? A soldier has to do a soldier's bidding; it's not for him to stop and think. I had her name from her mother who still mourns her loss those years ago. It was my duty to find her out and bring her home. Anything else was beyond the considerations of that limited redemption, the only one I was empowered to make. In any case, if that warrior loves her so much, why didn't he offer to come with her? He could live with both children and wife in a Christian setting, where she could be united with loved ones on both sides. If there are other people on his side, why don't they come with him too? Even now, if she wants me to, understanding her story like I couldn't have before she'd told it, I'll gladly delay our journey to send back for them. I'll wait here for word of their decision whatever it might be: to stay or to follow."

Mansilla, ignoring his subordinate officer, paces up and down beside that same fire and launches simultaneously into a monologue.

"The campfire is our army's democratic tribune," he says, "and now this formerly voiceless woman, who afterwards will be forgotten by her government and history, has spoken at it herself and made her voice heard as if she were a queen. I've learned so much on this journey! And now from her I'm still receiving instruction! If you'd told me before that this excursion to the Indians was going to teach me to understand humanity, I'd have answered with a Homeric laugh. Yet all our judgments are like that: imperfect like our very nature. Like Gulliver on his voyage to Lilliput, on my journey to the Ranquels I've seen the world exactly as it is. We're some pitiful devils, too. The dwarves have taken the giants' measure and the savages have taken ours. Nevertheless, here we are in this great America of ours, fancying ourselves so advanced and progressive. While, thanks to our noble efforts, civilization and liberty have ruined everything. In our recent war against Paraguay, we practically wiped that poor country out of existence, the latest statistic after the war yielding the number of a hundred and forty thousand women and fourteen thousand men. And we've accomplished this great work with Brazil. Between the two of us we've sent the tyrant López to the 'defunctory.' And now, since we're at war ourselves in our own province of Entre Ríos, we comfort ourselves with the thought that it'll soon be over. And that since Entre Ríos was very rich, it was time that it become acquainted with poverty. Spare the rod and spoil the child. That's the beginning of another rich sorrow."

That yellow moon, glimpsed briefly from amidst the fog, caresses with its gleaming light those individual speakers' solitudes. You, Dorotea, looking up from your own silence, seem struck too by a number of new or unfinished thoughts. It becomes evident that you're not yet finished speaking.

Chapter 18

Invented feminist discourse, fragment #1

Let me tell the good captain something about a woman's own mind, or a child's, for that matter. Cause whilst the captain pretends we don't neither of us have one, my experience tells me we do.

Someday, he says, I'll see it's all for the good, like he knows better'n me what that is, like I don't good 'n' well know what I think. He says, but he doesn't explain why, it was his duty to tell me what I ought to think. So he's treating me like some "mere child" that doesn't have a mind of her own, or like a beat-up captive who's too confused to remember what she used to think. Like since I gave myself to an Indian warrior, let myself be dirtied by some filthy savage, I can't see clear what a Christian man's love could be like, a Christian man that's got white skin like me and that's got the right religion.

But I did see that; he was killed once upon a time by my Christian father that wanted to keep me from him. He was reborn in the warrior that snatched me away from that sorrow, and again in the one that gave me my children.

And those children, they've suckled at my breasts and took their first steps right next to me. They've got from me a bit of that way of thinking and grown minds all their own. That part they didn't get from me? That's a gift from their beautiful father and from Cuchauentrú, who doesn't do no harm to His children but gives them the whole earth. His main gift's that free will or mind you see in them from the time of birthing. It's that mind of their own that doesn't need no one else saying what it. . . .

Chapter 19

Invented feminist discourse, fragment #2

. . .bout those crocodile tears of his. Maybe they're real, maybe they're not. All I know is they swallow up every bit of my womanly will. He acts all pitying for me losing my children. Everyone knows children belong by their mother. But his soldierly rules keep him from doing anything for them, even saving them from their savage father. He acts like he'd almost cry, like he has to keep this manly stone-face or his men'll think he's too weak to lead them. But all this crying and moaning doesn't do me no good without real mercy. Real mercy would have been to turn around somewhere that first part of the journey and set me free, let me go where my own will takes me. Real mercy'd be sending me back to those children, saving them from a mother's abandonment. And all his good feelings are useless to me if he hates the very life I'd choose for myself, the very husband I'd choose to spend it with. That's why I can't shed no tears for him when he talks about me offending *him*. Calling me ungrateful when it's he stripped *me* of almost all I had to be grateful for. What's he given me that I should lick his boots? I don't lick no man's boots. My true love wouldn't ever of ask. . . .

Chapter 20

Invented feminist discourse, fragment #3

. . .man's — or a soldier's — duty. Listen to this, all you men. It's not a man's duty to follow anyone's orders that, without damn good reason, take away some other's freedom. Cause that's what freedom means: my rights running alongside your rights, up until they mess with each other's. When they do mess with each other, when what I want goes against what you want, doesn't neither of us have the right to tell the other what to do. If you want me to live in one place and love whoever you say, whilst I want everything opposite of that, it's your duty to respect my wanting and let it alone. Same way with me. If I want you to live where I say and love who I say, whilst you want everything opposite, it's my duty to respect your wanting and just give you some gentle teaching if I think you're wrong. If you still don't want to follow me, that's your choice. The choice about me should be mine, too. Even if you think I'm wrong. God judge between me and you if I am, but He gave me freedom and you don't have no manly duty to take it a. . . .

Chapter 21

Invented feminist discourse, fragment #4

. . .be forced to give up all my wanting just cause you say it's for the best? I was born a free being. To live free, I chose the loneliness of these pampas. These pampas are where I want to stay, where my soul always will, no matter what you do. That's why I spit on your hateful offer. I won't let the ones I love be stole away with me. They're not *winca*, they've got no *winca* names. You keep on calling me that name that's not mine no more, and carrying me off where I don't belong no more neither. But I'll just keep on being who I am, not who you say I should be. I live here inside this love, this freedom, this loneliness I chose myself.

Epilogue:

The Romantic postlude that Mansilla (if it was Mansilla) forgot

[April, 2001]

Dear Leeza,

Just imagine the yellow moon emerging at last from the fog that's still rising off of the pond called La Verde. The frogs still croak their lonely chorus, an occasional bird swooping overhead in its slow, graceful descent toward the water. A single woman, rising by herself in that darkness and moving decisively toward the pond's southern dune, gracefully allows the moonlight to show her the way.

Stirring at the dwindling fire and looking sleepily around, the captain notices her absence. He rises to give pursuit, quickly. But just as he's about to give a general shout to those others to join in with him, he encounters the outstretched sword of his colonel. That pampean Don Quixote, who is firmly committed to preventing any action of his or any man's who might interfere with that brave woman's freely exercised will to flight.

Reluctantly, letting out a sigh that would seem to have carried away his whole soul, the captain sits down again and returns to pondering those mysteries that even then so stubbornly escape his understanding.

The shadow of that fleeing woman, returning to the land that at once holds both her promise and her doom, is joined on the horizon by that of an Indian warrior who's waiting there for her, four smaller shadows clutching tenderly at his legs.

With heart aflutter,

Vivi

The Prince and His Father

El Inca, con el odio que a la mala condición de su hijo tenía, no quiso admitir los consejos que sus parientes le daban; antes dijo que no se había de hacer caso del dicho de un loco furioso. . .

Hating his son's bad condition as he did, the Inca refused to give heed to the counsels of his relatives; he said, rather, that he wasn't going to pay attention to the words of a raving lunatic. . .

Inca Garcilaso de la Vega (1539-1616),
Comentarios Reales de los Incas
(Royal Commentaries of the Incas)

To Jonathan,
my Prince Viracocha

I wanted to write this story for you
when you were Pacha's age;
it just took me a while
to find the way.

The Prince and His Father

Pacha was lying face down across the width of his bed, in total darkness, when Viviana, his mother, knocked on the door. She let herself in and hit the light switch. Sleek black hair, loose and wild, fell across both shoulders and a third of the way down the boy's back. It hid his face. Sobbing violently, he shook beneath the earthquake that was his rage and his humiliation. He heard the slamming of a car door and the crunch of tires on gravel and snow as his father backed out of their long driveway toward the pot-holed, asphalt two-lane that would take him to his evening class at the private college across the interstate.

He felt the bed move as his mom plopped down beside him on the bedspread. She was lying there facing this lug of a fifteen-year-old man-child as she had always done after these tantrums when he was younger, to help him come down from that bad place as she could still occasionally (but less frequently) do. He felt her fresh breath against a fragment of exposed ear. With one hand, she tucked his hair behind it and softly stroked his cheek with her fingers. With the other hand, she propped up her head, elbow pressed against the woven outline of an Andean peak, mere centimeters from outstretched wings and beak of a soaring condor.

"He hates me. He wishes I was never born."

"Don't be silly. I saw in his eyes, when he first held you, how much he adores you."

"Adored me. Now he hates me."

"But why do you keep reacting so violently? You should know he was only trying to counsel you. Because you're his son and he worries about you."

"He loved me when I was little. I wasn't me, then. He didn't know me. Now all he does is yell."

"I don't excuse your father for his temper, Pacha. But you don't have to provoke him."

"You always take his side!" Pacha turned to face his mom, pulling himself up into his most accusing posture. He was a cat with its back up, ready to pounce. "Why don't you just admit he hates me?"

The rage flashed in his eyes. His voice was rising. He saw her looking back at him, recognized the hurt he was putting on her face, but still could not stop himself from whatever it was his invading demons would tell him to do.

"He's a good man, Pachito. If only you could try harder to remember that."

"See? Always taking his side! Always defending him!"

"To remember how you loved. . . ."

But Pacha was already on his feet, hearing nothing, looking around desperately for something to inflict the explosion of his anger on. He focused on the shelves with their mixture of books, trinkets, and art. Beside and partially facing a childish watercolor with a bright, blue ribbon on it, he saw the picture that some anonymous attendee at the arts program had taken of his scrawny self just short years ago, during one of his last moments at the grade school in Albuquerque, before the move east and far to the north, into the heart of America. There his once-piddling self stood, grinning stupidly inside the frame, behind the glass.

He held up the painting with its fanciful parade of jaguar, parrot, lion, boa constrictor, giraffe, llama, a crocodile tail in front and elephant trunk behind to suggest an infinity of the animal kingdom in either direction. Above them rose a stridently green canopy of Amazonian trees; while, yet further off, suspended in the sky like the conquistadors' pearly heaven, the glimmering Incan ruins of Machu Picchu presided at the height of those frigid Andes.

And there he stood, Zachary Pachacutec Garza-Suárez, a. k. a. Pacha, or Pachito, sometimes even Zach (by some semi-accommodating adult, stiff authoritarian figure who would never dream of addressing a minor by a nickname), or any number of choice bywords, depending on who was doing the calling.

There he was, anyway, at the height of his elementary-school glory: on one side, his prim and proper Norman Rockwellish teacher, her gray hair up in a towering bun; on the other, his olive-skinned mother, thirty-something daughter of immigrant parents from cosmopolitan Buenos Aires; and behind, hands resting firmly on the honoree's shoulders, his father, the dark-complexioned Peruvian American with chiseled Inca face, midway between forty and fifty.

All of them smiling like laughing hyenas on African savannas. Pacha's fury boiled over at the spectacle.

"I hate him!" he screamed. "I hate you, too! I hate. . . ."

And hating himself along with everyone else in this miserable North American wilderness in which he was captive, he grabbed the offending objects from the perch where they mocked him and threw them against the opposite wall. Suddenly, right next to each other, the frames turned face-up on the floor, he knelt over them and pounded — explosively, self-destructively, volcanically — he pounded and pounded and pounded. His closed fists slammed repetitively against their protective, now savaging glass.

He tore off translucent shards and seized both painting and photograph from the wreckage. His mother, pleading, arms thrown around him, clutched at his wrists to hold them back.

"You can't stop me! I hate you! You can't stop me!"

Knuckles and fingers bleeding, elbows swinging, he knocked her onto her back, ripped himself clear of her, and tore the self-sacrificial images into crimson shreds. Then he gave himself over to crying. Viviana Suárez-Garza, long-suffering mother, pulled herself to her knees and embraced him, crying softly in counterpoint to his violent sobs. Arms tight around him, she rocked him ever so slightly, shushing and humming, until he entered that almost comatose zombie state that told her he was calm and posed no immediate threat to either one of them.

She led him across the hall, to medicine cabinet and sink, where she would spend the next good while picking splinters of glass from his bloodied skin and disinfecting and bandaging him as best she could.

"You're so exasperating," she said in scarcely a whisper, breaking through the silence that hung over them like a suffocating fog. "Oh, Pachito. My little world-shaker. My precious *diablo*. What am I going to do with you?"

Afterwards, while he sat uncommunicative in the spot she had guided him to in the living room, she put on some Andean flute music and prepared him a hot coca tea with the same curative and pain-relieving agents as the nonnarcotic paste that she had placed on his wounds.

Viviana Suárez, married to Garza, saddled with their impossible child, positioned herself — legs crossed — on the floor near the unsettled prince. She sat erect and quiet, with the serene posture of the sacred Pachamama, cosmic earth goddess of time and fertility. And resting there, immovable, she waited.

When Jorge finally arrived home, their devil-child with the angelic face and piercing green eyes slept soundly on the couch. Viviana, in that meditative pose, had started to nod off herself. When she looked up at her husband, he saw her tear-stained face and sad smile, envisioned her brooding over cosmic waters like some apocryphal, Semitic goddess-hen on fertile eggs.

She cocked her head slightly and pointed her eyes toward the light down the hall that she had forgotten to turn off. She offered Jorge her hand and he helped her up. She stood over him, at the end of the hallway, at light's threshold as he squatted there holding the jagged edge of a sunlit corner of Machu Picchu.

One eyelid twitched as he glanced back over his shoulder, through a light gauze of mist, at the mother of his only son.

"Our untameable young prince, Virachocha," she said. "What do we do for him?"

~*~

While Viviana had sat nearby in her yogic pose — Meditative Pachamama or Serenity Buddha — Pacha visited primeval childhood in a dream-web. He dreamt his mother ensconced in mountain flora. Her body was snugly tucked into forest and fields, cultivated or speckled with the local fauna. Head and hands, palms pressed together in calming prayer, emerged from crag and escarpment. Her earthen brown face, encircled by green and fecund scarf, lit the land like a Bedouin's smiling oasis.

She beamed at him, her world-shaking Viracocha, rebellious and blessed with courage and light, in spite of the ferocity of his young heart.

Ay, m'hijo, she sang, *my wild, savage boy. What am I gonna do with you till your time comes?*

She stood up, shaking the foliage from waist and thighs, skirts flying as she swung him about in a solitary orbit around its warming Sun.

His father, in cartoonish Incan attire, extended Sun's golden rays. Pacha danced on one until it gave way beneath his jagged demigod's feet. Downward he swooped, arms outstretched like the sacred condor's, only down and down like a meteor bound on destruction, on a hopeless course of self-annihilation. He circled earthward, in tighter and tighter loops until they formed the lethal gradient of a straight, vertical line.

Gaia's hard surface is flying up to me, he thought in stoical acceptance. *She's an impenetrable, rocky surface. I'll be shattered against her like a crystal chandelier against the bottom of the unsinkable Titanic; or like the crushing, icy thunderbolt that slew arrogant Cronus.*

As he plunged, the skin melted off Pacha's face and his teeth rattled like death in rhythmic, skeletal disintegration. His scream pierced the barrier of all sound, dissipated into time and space. It was sucked into the black hole of his fear and his rage.

~*~

"Hey, Geronimo!" some pasty town boy called from down and across the hall a ways. "What's with the bandages?"

"Nah," his friend shouted over random chatter and slamming lockers. "I bet it's Mohammad. The Injun get-up's a disguise. Raghead terrorist burnt his hands making some explosive device to blow us all up with."

"Or else he really is a Injun," Pasty-Boy answered, his high-pitched laugh like a whining puppy or a squealing piglet. "Got a tomahawk in his backpack. Gonna scalp him the whole kit 'n' caboodle."

Pacha, fuming inside and gritting his teeth, kicked the metal door shut and turned up the sound on his ear pods. He smirked as the tough-as-nails history teacher came out of her classroom and started chewing on the big-mouths. His knuckles still throbbed as he slipped into her class empty-handed.

Ms. Quincey strode through the open door and straight to Pacha's desk. His eyes were closed; he nodded to the electric rhythms. She tugged at the pod in his left ear and signaled for him to give up the contraband.

"Mr. Zachary P. Garza." She looked at him sternly, palm extended. "Where are your supplies?"

"Can't do any work today. Probably for another week or two. Tore my hands up wrestling a coyote last night, but don't worry. I saved the chickens."

His classmates laughed. He winked at the pale-skinned, black-haired Goth-girl in front who had turned to face him, a glimmer of mischief in her eyes. Ms. Quincey looked him over mordantly and turned away.

"Too bad. A little more pain never hurt a noble warrior like you. Now open your ears and borrow what you need. And don't let me see you come to class again without those supplies."

In the opening conversation about current events, talk turned to the new resistance movement taking shape up on the Canadian border against yet another pipeline.

"More power to them. I hope they win," said one boy.

"Police should take care of them just like they done the rabble-rousers out at Standing Rock," a thickset girl with an NRA T-shirt shot back.

"You'd like that, wouldn't you?" Pacha muttered under his breath. "Long as you've got your second amendment so you can shoot anyone with half a brain."

"What's that, Patch-of-'Paca-Crap? Got something to say to me, you pack of crap?"

"That'll be quite enough—"

Ms. Quincey had barely opened hers when Pacha jumped in with his big mouth and ecological conscience.

"Yes. I do. What about their right to freely assemble and peaceably protest, Dumb Butt?"

"Yeah," Goth-Girl pitched in. "What about that?"

But that's exactly what they'll do, Pacha thought. Brute force wins out every time. They'll send in the frickin' Marines if they have to. Land of the free, my ass.

~*~

On a still, cold night in the middle of January, Pacha and his parents were camped out under a light, steady snowfall. Unwilling prisoner in these northern wildlands, he had nevertheless pitched his own tent and painstakingly assembled the structure of wood that became the present fire. In the clearing where they sat huddled around those flames on canvas folding chairs, heads covered by knitted Peruvian chollo hats pulled down over their ears, Viviana addressed her male audience, in particular the youngest.

"I was just thinking about what the Inca Garcilaso told about your namesake, Viracocha."

Pacha turned his head away from her and his father. He stared dully into the dancing flames.

"Not that crap again. And he's not my namesake."

"Practically. Just two aliases for the same guy."

"Why'd you have to name me that, anyway? Patch-of-You-Know-What. Might as well just call me Shithead."

"Sorry," Jorge said. "We didn't foresee that. Should have gone with Viracocha."

"Or Prince. Prince Viracocha Garza."

"Then it would be Veera-*Caca* or something. Veera-Caca from Lake Titty-Caca. Zach would have done just fine."

"I'm sorry, Pachito, but this too shall pass."

"And before you know it."

Saying so, persisting bravely in the paternal role of encourager and counselor, Jorge reached over to pat his griping son on the shoulder. Pacha jerked away from his touch. He went on talking.

"I tried to get everyone to just call me Zach. But there's always some stupid sub, stumbling all over the whole monstrosity. Or you, Mom, just blurting it out. In case someone's forgot."

Jorge sighed. He stood up and took a few paces, eyes flashing, eyelid twitching. Then, after poking uselessly at the fire, he sat down on a log on the other side of it.

"So." For Jorge's sake, Viviana tried to hide the laughter in her voice. "Getting back to your favorite story, Zachary. The one that got us off on this sad lament of yours."

"Crap."

"Since it revolves around an impatient old geezer-king and his rambunctious young prince, I dedicate this incarnation of it to you and your dad. But especially, *m'hijo*, to the chivalrous young knight hiding behind those sour looks."

And when it's time, she thought in her maternal heart, *you'll teach it to me in its true, twenty-first-century configuration. Then I'll set it on the shelf beside Dorotea.*

~*~

"It all began, my darling Pachacutec, little earth-shaper, precious *diablito*, master illusionist with the power or potentiality to make the world over — it all began in a sacred space high in the Andes; where the Sun's new children could live in peace, in a place destined for a people who would never be completely devoured, whose legacy would remain intact until whenever others might come, from their various lands, to awaken the old spirits."

Thus spoke the mother to her man-child, the reincarnated Inca American prince — Viracocha; sometimes called Pachacutec — child of earth and sun and stars.

That other tale, the tale of Dorotea-the-captive, which his mother got published before he was born or even thought of, Pacha had recently read in its formal, written version. Previously, whenever she told it to him, she would narrate more simply, each time with whatever subtractions or elaborations as occurred to her, but without the postmodern structure and ironic intrusions of her millennial perspective. At those times he seemed to recall drifting in and out of it as he lay in bed, slipping back and forth into the netherworld between wakefulness and sleep. Sometimes he would awake on the other side of that frontier, alone and lost in the fog of his subconscious.

This newly re-fashioned story is another matter. Its origins were much more ancient than the nineteenth-century folklore of Dorotea Bazán, that twice-captive woman who is said to have rebelled at being rescued, against her will, from her adopted Indian family on the Argentine pampas. This one, first written down in the fifteen hundreds by the Inca Garcilaso de la Vega, son of a Spanish conquistador and an Inca princess, originates still earlier in the mists of Indigenous legend and mythology — in the Imperial Incan capital of Cuzco, in present-day Perú, where the chronicler was born.

"It began," Viviana went on, "in a blessed day when Our Father the Sun set two of his children down — the first Inca, Manco Cápac and his queen, Mama Huaco Ocllo — on what is now the Peruvian side of Lake Titicaca."

"Titty Caca," Pacha said. He snorted, affecting an indifferent, sarcastic laugh. Viviana, smiling softly, otherwise ignored him.

"He put them there," she continued, "so that they could bring light and culture to the Indians of those heights and valleys, who were an indecent and barbarous sort. The rest, as they say, is legend, with a sprinkling of mythology and fable along the way.

"But the greatest of days came in the time of the Inca called Yáhuar Huácac and the rebellious prince, his son, who would live to be by far the greater of the two."

Viviana added this aside, with a wink and a nod across the fire to her husband: "With sincerest apologies to my man, to my darkling Peruvian hombre, who is undoubtedly the finest of all living"; though she winked, in turn, contradictorily, at his son and rival.

Jorge, still smarting from his son's latest rejection, twisted up his face in a sort of anguished grimace posing as a smile. He muttered under his breath a pair of choice words that he half wished his slyly mocking wife would hear. Smirking at the perceived insult to his father, meanwhile, Pacha fell into a distracted attention. At the same time, as his mother launched into the narrative, diving in beyond that annoying dedication, thoughts of freedom already lay heavy and earnest on Pacha's rebellious mind.

"Yáhuar Huácac, you might say, was a peaceful man with bloody eyes — at least in his infancy, since the Indians said he'd been seen crying blood when he was just starting to walk. More likely, Garcilaso sensibly tells us, this happened in childbirth when he emerged from his mother's womb bearing some of her placenta. Be that as it may, that's how he got that name — Bloody Tears, you could translate it — and how it came to be rumored, because of a prophecy associated with that incident, that some evil would afflict his government.

"Superstitious fellow that he was, anyway, Bloody Tears was afraid to leave the streets of Cuzco or even to stray far from the royal precinct. He treated his people with the same justice, compassion, and gentleness that was the gold standard among the ruling Incas, but he wasn't as bold as his predecessors. Bottom line: he was afraid to lead the king's horses and lead the king's men — or men and llamas, maybe?" (her laughter rang out against the cold, wintry silence) "— into fearsome and unequal combat.

"But in spite of his unwavering patience with all the most lowly of his subjects — and this remains a common ailment, among men who lead or teach — the Crying Emperor had none left over for his son. Yáhuar Huácac was troubled by the un-Inca-like brusqueness of the boy's nature. From the time of his childhood, the unruly prince had acted quite the bully among other children, throwing his weight around like a future tyrant. Since in his adolescence he still seemed inclined to the same cruelties, showing no signs whatsoever of submitting to counsel, the angry father banished him to the countryside.

"So, rather than a training appropriate for one destined to inherit the throne, to inherit the godly title itself, in his solitude the future Inca herded his father-the-king's sheep. For several years, no one heard a peep from him."

"You'd like that, wouldn't you, Dad?"

"Why do you say that, my darling boy?"

Pacha ground his teeth together at the infuriating sound of his father's dripping irony. His eyes shot razors at the man across the fire. He felt his own father's anger like a bolt of electricity to his nervous system. Zeus's thunderbolt sliced downward from tip of head through narrow trunk toward the navel, dividing his top half into a layered canopy drooping with icy leaves. He saw the rage burning in his father's eyes. He wanted to leap across the flames and have at him. He felt the tug where the umbilical cord used to be, its ghostly remnant still tying him — protectively — to his Pachamama.

"Remember the time when you pulled off the road somewhere out West toward Navajo country? Up against the mountains where we could see the shepherd boy with his flock? Because I'd sassed back to you one too many times, and so you tossed me out of the car and told me to go herd some sheep?"

"I remember," Jorge growled. "If your mother hadn't objected, it might have even done you some good."

"Yeah, I saw you try to leave me there. I saw you start driving off and then Mom laying into you, slapping you around in that old rattrap on wheels. I knew she'd make you come back for me. I was laughing my head off when you swerved off into the dust and made that big U-turn. I could still hear her screaming when you pulled over and told me to get the hell in."

Jorge, cowed by the memory of her tears and his shame, glanced at her sheepishly and hung his head.

"You do know, I presume, that I wasn't really going to leave you there for good. Just wanted to get your attention."

"Boys, boys," Viviana interrupted. "Shall we leave old dogs to lie and get back to our story?"

A hint of sadness cloaked the laughter that Pacha saw still spilling from her mouth like brightly colored stars. He vaguely heard his father sigh.

Then she spoke of how the Inca's son, changed by the experience of so much solitude and reflection, came to him with an uncanny message. He told his father, bowing humbly in his presence, of how a strange figure, bearded and with a long robe nearly reaching his feet, had appeared to him while he was guarding Their Father the Sun's sheep.

"Whether I was awake or sleeping I can't be sure," the young prince said, "but I tell you in all earnestness that he spoke to me."

Then Viviana went on to relate how the divine being, who called himself Inca Viracocha, told the prince to warn his father of a gathering army that intended to topple him from his throne and destroy the imperial city.

"But this Emperor of the Bloody Eyes," Viviana said,

"blinded by his earlier disappointment in his raucous boy, chose not to believe him. Although his counselors pointed out that it would have been a terrible blasphemy to invent such things, a sin unthinkable even to a rebellious prince, Yáhuar Huácac cast his son back out from his presence. He would hear nothing more of the matter. So, within three months, when the royal forces finally confirmed that an army thirty-thousand warriors strong was coming against the city, the venerable Inca found himself unprepared and, like a scaredy-cat, whatever his other virtues had been, determined that he couldn't mount a strong resistance at such a late moment and chose, therefore, tail between his legs, to flee the city, abandoning it to its fate."

~*~

Stomping several yards into the woods from their camp in the clearing, Pacha stood listening to the crash of his insistent waters on the yellow leaves and snow.

Stupid father! As if no one can ever change. Like, wouldn't sending him out by himself in the wilderness give him time to think? Doesn't he think that can have an effect on someone? And on top of that, it's not like the old fart isn't at least part to blame in the first place. If he knew his son's heart — if he wasn't always provoking him, yelling and screaming at him, complaining about how he's not measuring up to some impossible standard — he could see what's plain to everyone else. He could see when his son's telling the truth, when he's got something real to say. But, no, not this doofus! Hope he's happy out there in the cold, all alone like that lion with the flying monkeys and his own frickin' cowardliness.

But what about his *own* stupid self, Pacha thought. He wanted to be closer to his father, but how could he talk to his father when he doesn't even know his own mind or thoughts? Everything's just insane, his life and the world and everyone in it. Maybe Pacha was as scared as that old king about the world and his future. His own generation doomed to melt away in the fires of Climate Armageddon, anyway. Nuclear or Climate Freakin' Armageddon! Born just in time for the final fireworks, the final shake-up. Nothing at all to do about it, piddly little punk that he is. Yet his mom wants him to think he's this latter-day Inca prince or something? Is she crazy?

But what if she isn't? What if his mom's the only sane one? Why, if she's not, is he getting so messed up by her story? And here he is, pissing up a yellow stream and freezing his willy in these leafless woods in the middle of winter. Hanging by the thread that says maybe — just maybe — she sees something that he still can't. Is it possible she really does? And not just some figment of willful imagining?

~*~

Jorge Garza had returned to Viviana — like a reproved child full of tender glances, pouty lips, and vows of repentance — from his self-exile on the other side of the campfire. She only briefly pretended to spurn his petition.

"I am always amazed by the power your words have on that boy," he said softly. "What is it, *¿cosa de mujer?* Just a woman's thing, *nomás?*"

Viviana Suárez, wife of Garza, smiled faintly and looked aslant at the fire. Against those flames she envisioned the silhouette of their troubled, gifted boy: only, in Incan garb, Prince Viracocha or Pachacutec, looking off in the distance at Andean peaks as if some wondrous thought might be taking hold of him.

"Or," Jorge said, "maybe a mother's thing. When I speak — I, his father — the Furies erupt."

"It wasn't always so. And some day it won't be, once again. Remember when he was little? How he hung, then, on *your* every word and action?"

"I can't see it, anymore. Do you really think so?"

Pachito's father shook his head. He was at once a melancholy and an impassioned man. He was torn between the creative and the destructive powers of his quantum physics, the forces that have made life so capricious and fragile, full of otherworldly possibilities and terrors. His wife's thought, like so many others, struck him in a sad way.

"And I," she added, "didn't quell his rage so well the other night, did I?"

"Because you spoke in my defense. If only I weren't involved."

Viviana Suárez, helpmate to Garza, nurturer as well to his son, took a sip of the hot yerba maté that had been passing between them. In a moment, once he had returned from his reverie in the woods, she would hand the silver gourd to Pacha.

"If only I could string more than two sentences together at a time, is the thing. Or talk of something that might strike him more personally. Ruffle his feathers, perhaps, but more importantly, wake him up to potentialities. To this promise you seem to never stop seeing in him."

"Leave his feathers alone, you silly man. Let him talk to you, instead, of his fears and his hopes. Tell him about your own when you were his age. Allow your words to take their proper place in his heart. Then just let it be, whatever will. Let it be."

Sitting there, Jorge suddenly remembered the first time he had heard her talk, the way she captivated him, then, beside the University of New Mexico Duck Pond where he summoned the courage to speak to her. The way she still did in this unlikely Midwestern sojourn.

"My wife, the sage," he said dreamily. "Mother of my son, midwife to my soul."

~*~

"The inhabitants of the city, finding themselves thus forsaken, also began fleeing — willy-nilly, as they say in these parts, or, helter-skelter, in whichever directions they could," Viviana said with her characteristic laugh.

"Some of them came across the banished prince — Inca Viracocha, is the title they would come to know him by — and told him what had happened. Greatly distressed by what his father had done, he first commanded those present to spread the word that whoever wanted to save the city should follow him. Then, intercepting his father on his shameful retreat, he reproved him for his cowardice and announced, to those royal attendants with him, that they, too, if they didn't want to share in the father's disgrace, should join the son who would help them to redeem their city."

Jorge, pensive and chastened by his wife's most recent counsel, stirred at this vision of what their own son, perhaps, could yet become.

"Viracocha's conduct here really is praiseworthy," he said.

He paused briefly to gauge Pacha's receptiveness. Uncertain, but not encountering any visible resistance, he continued.

"I wonder, though, about the father. What shame he

must have felt. Not only for letting his people down because of his obstinate refusal to listen, but for his utter failure at raising a son. At trusting him to grow in wisdom."

"And I wonder," Viviana said, "if that's the real source of his cowardice in this moment."

"But he was afraid to even leave the city!" Pacha exclaimed. "He was a coward from the beginning."

"Maybe he feels that, too. That if he'd projected strength like his ancestors did, these invaders wouldn't have felt so emboldened. And so his failure with his son — as you just said, Jorge — maybe that made him feel doubly a coward for just throwing him aside like that, when he himself hadn't been fully an Inca."

"And then," Jorge said — he smiled at his perpetually young bride, at his rescuer (from himself) now and on so many occasions — "and then, faced with that self-knowledge, that brutal knowledge that slapped him in the face like the driving wind of the Andean plateau, that failure consumed him and he lost hope."

Viviana, looking from him to their son, head tilted slightly in his own reluctant grappling to understand, spoke once more: "And how, in that case, could he do anything but despair?"

"So, fine!" the ponderer spoke. "But if I was him I think I'd rather die. Even if he just waits there, doing nothing, waiting for the spear that finally pierces his heart."

"True," Jorge conceded. "And that action, however feeble, would have shown a modicum of courage, perhaps."

After the silence, after that discussion had clearly run its course, the storyteller continued her self-appointed labor. She spoke of the enemy's crossing of the Apurímac

River, last obstacle on their approach to Cuzco; but also of their own army which had by then grown to some eight thousand men. And she spoke of how, among those Indians who had gathered behind Prince Viracocha, were the Quechuas, whose ancient enemies now threatened the royal city.

"Regional bullies who had been such a royal pain in their collective ass," Viviana laughed. "No way were they going down without a fight. No way were the Quechuas easily going to submit, once more, to those wretched tyrants."

She spoke then of young Prince Viracocha's gestures of peace. If they would lay down their weapons and submit peacefully to the Incas' generous and rational governance, he would grant them full pardon on behalf of his father, Yáhuar Huácac. But in their dark pride, the deadly hubris of mythical Greek tyrants across centuries and distant seas, and seeing the father in flight, they weren't inclined to pay much heed to the son.

"Tomorrow," they sent in haughty reply, "it will be seen who deserves to be king and can pardon offenses."

"Pitiful fools," Viviana sang in her lilting voice, "because what followed would not be pretty. The battle soon commenced, and it was bloody on both sides. On and on it raged, neither side gaining an advantage, though the young prince's army was being constantly sustained by a continual trickle of fresh forces that were coming to his defense from all the surrounding regions.

"Knowing that his Inca ancestors were always quick to exaggerate their accomplishments with fables and tall tales," she told, "Prince Viracocha was quick to take advantage of that stream of reinforcements to intimidate the enemy. Those arrogant invaders were becoming confused and frustrated by that unceasing flow of defenders.

"So the prince and his champions started noising about that, because the Sun and God Viracocha so commanded, the very rocks and shrubs of those fields were changing into men and coming to fight in the service of the Incan Empire."

She paused for a moment and surveyed her tiny audience. She laughed outright at the absurdity of the tale.

"Those rumors had their desired effect," she said. "The enemy was vanquished. And it's said that the blood flowed like water through the bed of a dry creek in that region. Afterwards the place came to be known as Yáhuar Pampa, or Bloody Field."

A sliver of yellow moon shone down against the shadow cast by a tree. The audience seemed lost in thought.

"Pity the fools!" growled Pacha, miming the discordant gestures of Mr. T. He smiled when his father, the first to acknowledge the mimicry of his mother's borrowed words, laughed heartily and nodded in his direction.

"So I've still got your attention, I see."

"Good one, son."

Viviana, pleased to see that smile plastered all over the boy's youthful face, paused for a few more seconds to study it.

"Listen, rogues. The story presses onward," she said after a while, beginning at once to describe the dressing-down that Prince Viracocha gave to his subdued enemies. "He told them to give thanks to the Sun, who commanded his children to treat Indians with mercy. For that reason, he pardoned their lives and returned them to their homes, even though they deserved death at his hands.

"Given young Viracocha's reputation," she went on, "the Indians who had fought for him were surprised by his merciful attitude. They figured that the Sun must have transformed his character, making him over to be more like the Incas who'd preceded him.

"For his part, having visited the city and shown that he was its humble lord, the young prince went out to the rebellious territories to make sure they were well governed by his representatives. Then, walking on foot to show that he was, first of all, a soldier, he returned to Cuzco. Only afterwards did he again leave the city to visit his father, who didn't welcome him with the rejoicing and happiness that such a great feat deserved, but with a grave and pained expression."

"At least," Pacha interrupted, "he should throw himself at Viracocha's feet. Beg his forgiveness for all he'd done."

"And failed to do," said the father. "I know."

"Be that as it may," the smiling storyteller said. "However, no one but those two men witnessed their secret conference."

Jorge objected. "In that case, how do you know the father received him with nothing but that somber expression? Maybe he greeted him with tears of joy at his feat, mixed with humility and sorrow at his failure. He might have done exactly what Pacha said he should do."

"Ask Garcilaso, if you must," she said in her melodious voice. "I'm just telling it the way the Inca Garcilaso put it down on parchment. But the end result was that the father would remain in self-exile outside of the city he'd abandoned. Prince Viracocha didn't remove his father's crown, however, but took one of his own instead. And from that moment, he began governing the kingdom he'd saved. His acts, in the rest of his days, were great and many."

Viviana went on from there to tell of a significant encounter that followed on the fame of those innumerable deeds. Finding himself at some distance from Cuzco, Viracocha received ambassadors from the kingdom of Tucma, which the Spaniards would call Tucumán. It was located at some two hundred leagues from the royal province, on the borders of what became her son's maternal ancestors' Argentina.

As the Quechuas had in an earlier time, they begged to come under the kindly rule of the Incas. Their boundaries had already begun to spread into regions as far north as Quito, in Ecuador, approaching the border with Colombia; and into Chile, in the south, touching upon the lands of that unconquerable race of Araucanians who were forebears of Viviana's twice-captive Dorotea's Ranquel Indians on the Argentine pampas.

"On the other hand, my darling Pachacutec, you who are also a child of Perú, your namesake the Inca Viracocha was deeply saddened by the melancholy story — related to him on another of his travels — of the valiant Hancohuallu. While having spent the last decade under the same gentle rule that the Tucmas came seeking, he secretly gathered those of his former subjects who would follow and escaped across mountains toward an unknown land. There he intended to govern alone, his proud spirit unable to suffer being subject or vassal of another."

Viviana paused for a moment, as if to let the sadness of that peculiar thirst for an obstinate, selfish freedom to rule sink in.

~*~

There are so many different freedoms, Pacha thought as his mother fell silent. *It's almost like, if you're free, someone else has to be a slave.*

His nemesis Miss Second Amendment's right to bear arms, it occurred to him, her right to own guns in the sacred name of the Constitution, was freedom only to turn around and oppress others' constitutional rights to protest the rampant violence and injustice in American society: against abused women and gunned-down schoolchildren; against Muslims and Blacks and all the other people of color; against the poor, the marginalized, the unwanted immigrant; against the least whiff of "socialist" or "commie" ideology or any kind of liberal thought.

Except, as his father would now and then declaim over an evening's dinner, when he wasn't lambasting his son, *neo*liberal economics or rampant, unregulated, laissez-faire capitalism.

But also, Pacha wondered, reflecting on his mother's recounting of those last two opposed and enigmatic tales, what about all those lesser, more primitive Indian nations who found freedom under the apparent enslavement of their supposedly benevolent Inca overlords? Was it even possible that any imperial power be so remarkably merciful and generous to the subdued and pacified masses? Or that they all be so thoroughly subdued and pacified in the first place?

And what about the long arm of his own American Empire? Whose freedom were we actually fighting for across the Mediterranean, he wanted to know. And how many enemy-civilian deaths would it take, to paraphrase an old folk song that his mom and his grandmom used to always like singing to him when he was little — how many deaths would it take before we let what was left of them be free?

Or something like that: the answer still blowing on an ever-changing, hurricane-force, world-ravaging wind.

But this Incan story of father and son? Even that was beginning to take hold of him in some way. As it still hadn't, even those two years ago when his mother told it to him on the long haul from Albuquerque.

God forbid that he show it too much, at this moment in this particular space, but suddenly — despite all resistance and anger — he was aware of himself beginning, not just to listen, but to hear.

~*~

After her moment, Viviana went on. Her voice became lazy and remote, as if she were dreaming. Her narrative was all but finished.

"Our hero, the young Inca Viracocha," she said, "grew old in his time and was succeeded by his son, that Inca Pachacutec — his namesake, too, according to some — who was justly famed for his many laws and proverbs, as well as for conquests of his own. And Pachacutec, in his turn, was followed by a brief succession of others. The last of those was the enigmatic figure of Atahualpa, whom Pizarro and his Spanish troops captured and cruelly executed.

"Garcilaso seems to condemn Atahualpa. He claims he was only a pretender to the throne that by rights belonged to another. Be that as it may. But to me, he remains a fitting symbol of that whole magnificent empire that, with his betrayal and death, came abruptly to an end. I continually ponder its lessons of community and of liberty, each intertwined and dependent on the other."

~*~

After some further banter — at the last, there was Jorge's traditional campfire tale (but with an Andean twist) about things that go bump in the night — mother and father gathered their young charge from his premature slumber. One on either side, they walked him to the relative warmth of tent and sleeping bag. They collapsed, then, against each other's bodies within the larger space of their own tent, where she would try to probe the secrets of her husband's sadness, to soothe the vestiges of his sorrow.

Pacha dreamt, in the wee hours of the emergent morning, of a parade of exotic animals — a procession of Inca, Mesoamerican, African, and Polynesian kings, generations of demigods and goddesses — that extended from one end of the starry sky to the other. But then, startled awake in his dream by some sort of cosmic earthquake, his spirit self cried out in despair and horror. In the nightmare that ensued, that profusion of celestial beings dissolved into a contracting darkness that left them all — and himself — without air. He bolted up from where he was sleeping and stared all around himself at the infernal abyss. In this apocalyptic dreamscape, he heard himself scream. He was conscious, nevertheless, of the fact that no sound would emerge from his throat. He felt something like the existential pain of that willowy figure in the famous Expressionist painting by Edvard Munch. He couldn't move.

But his mother, assured of his ultimate triumph, dreamt prophetically of what she knew deep in her soul was yet to come; or, in some parallel quantum world, just the other side of a rip in the fabric of eternity, was happening now: a mystical being who, in that spirit realm, exemplified Pacha's secret yearnings, enacting his part in the sacred pageant that will be his destiny. As she awoke, her face shimmered with occult knowledge that sanctified his quest.

~*~

Pacha emerged from the school library with a burst of enthusiasm. He had just discovered Hiram Bingham's famous account of Machu Picchu. He came into the hallway carrying that book, another on Incan religion and myth, and his mother's copies of Garcilaso's *Royal Commentaries of the Incas* and the ecologically-conscious antipoems of the Chilean Nicanor Parra.

Rounding the corner, he stumbled over the deliberately-placed foot of an older boy. His books went flying. Pacha landed on his face and bled from the nose.

"Who the hell is this Inca dude?" one of his tormenters asked as he leafed carelessly through Garcilaso's book.

"The chief of some human sacrificers that some Spanish revenger — Señor Monte Zoomer, or something — conquered in Mexico," said his more astute companion as he stared at the hieroglyphic image on the cover of the book on myths. "Looks like our *Native American* friend, here, is boning up on all that heathen hocus-pocus."

"Shut your mouths and hand over the books," said the librarian. A passing teacher, meanwhile, helped Pacha off the floor, while a student stopped to rescue the other volumes.

"Go ahead, take 'em," one of the two stooges said.

"Only a real bonehead would read garbage like this," said the other as they headed along on their way.

One of them, Shakespearean clown with wit and one-liners, followed with something about nerd-boys and their nasty boners.

Moments later, as Pacha leaned back in the nurse's office with a wet washcloth against his nose, Goth-Girl came in to commiserate.

"Effin' losers. Worthless douchebags. I wouldn't give them another thought, if I was you."

"Tell that to my nose."

When the nurse hollered at her to get along to class, already, she leaned over and kissed Pacha on the cheek.

"Thanks, anyway. My nose thanks you, too."

"Bet that's not the only part of you that's thanking me," she said, nodding at the involuntary bulge starting to show in his pants.

Later, after school, some other losers heading for their cars caught them making out behind the building.

"Hiawatha and his ugly squaw," the funny one shouted. His friend burst into a peal of laughter and kept slapping the palm of his hand across his mouth. He made a noise they'd all learned on the playground, if not at home on the TV from pre-*Dances with Wolves* Westerns.

Goth-girl answered them with her middle finger and an abundantly creative stream of profanity, while Pacha just clenched his fists and burned with rage. In his mind he wanted to be the young Inca Viracocha, only this time with an automatic weapon like Weird Al Yankovic's reanimated Gandhi on that You Tube clip:

"No more Mr. Passive Resistance! He's out to kick some butt!"

~*~

Over the following weeks, as his parents conversed uneasily about the latest political and environmental protests around the country and world — and the consistently authoritarian responses to those populist rebellions — Pacha became increasingly agitated. He would rap his fingers at the dinner table; his legs jerked spasmodically beneath it.

Rivulets of icy water trickled between inches of compacted, melting snow on an uncommonly warm February morning. Inside, during the current-events discussion in Ms. Quincey's class, a frenzy of words erupted between Pacha and a trio of provocateurs that included the thick-set girl who had previously spoken in favor of attack dogs and stun grenades against water protectors and nonviolent resisters.

In the hallway after class, the volley of words became fists. Pacha got in a few punches before Miss NRA and her thickset male cousins laid him out on the floor.

Over dinner that evening, there was the expected fatherly inquisition.

"Five days suspension," Jorge repeated. "And *you* threw the first punch."

Pacha looked down at the spinach cannelloni that he had scarcely touched. He had cut it into small pieces and was pushing it around on his plate. Occasionally he took a bite, but hardly tasted it. Viviana had prepared it — her grandmother's Argentine recipe — because it was his favorite.

"And at a girl, no less."

"Call her that if you want, Dad. She's built like a bulldog and has the personality of a Rottweiler. And she's been hounding me for weeks. She was poking her finger in my side — poke, poke, poke; poke, poke, poke — and I'd had enough."

"So you punched her. How'd that turn out for you?"

"Jorge. Stop taunting him."

Pacha, turning his chair over violently as he went, marched out of the room. Before storming out the front door, he punched a hole in the drywall on one side of the entranceway.

"How'd that go for you?" Viviana hissed as she got up from her chair, then started clearing the table and banging around in the kitchen. "That's the way to get his feathers up, you big man. And just exactly what is it you think you've accomplished with that mighty feat of feather-ruffling, my dolt of a husband?"

Kicking and stomping around outside in the mud and muck, Pacha cussed a blue streak at the cawing crows and barking dogs. He broke off a low-hanging branch from a tree, sharpening its end with a rusted old pocket knife found in a ramshackle shed a quarter mile or so down the road, and sloshed about jousting at invisible demons like a deranged, Quixotic knight.

At last, acknowledging himself vanquished, he briefly contemplated the potential glory of falling on that spike, spilling his guts like some defeated king in ancient battle. Instead, he broke it across his knee. It probably wasn't sharp or strong enough for the job, anyway, he thought. Standing there beneath the moonlight, he tossed its fragments into the madding stream and watched them go.

As he stood there, basking in that otherworldly luminescence, something peculiar happened. It was almost as if a minute being of the Sun, some invisible quantum presence, walked out to him on that moonbeam and spread healing Andean balm across his forehead. Or perhaps some cosmic Incan dust was sprinkled in his hair, enveloping him from head to foot in a temporary, protective layer of invincibility.

It wasn't that he heard an actual voice, but the words somehow seemed to fill his consciousness as he came into a state of wakefulness that no person in mortal condition — in mere three-dimensional reality — could normally endure without being consumed in invisible flames. And the voice — or incandescent spirit, or serum, whatever it was — communicated to him that he should be at peace. His way would be blessed. Never mind whatever obstacles might yet appear to block his passage.

That presence must have withdrawn, then, laying him down gently on the wet ground. Because when Pacha awoke, he was being carried homeward in his earthly father's clumsy arms.

Jorge Garza was breathing heavily, feeling his way cautiously in the dark.

"It's okay, Pachito. You're my son, and I love you. We'll find our way together, somehow, out of this wilderness."

And a woman would lead them. At the threshold to their shelter, Viviana awaited, her hair aglow beneath a nimbus of moonlight.

In Search of Dorotea Bazán

or, On Breaking Out of Literary Isolation[1]

Summer, 1997. I had started to translate Mansilla ten or twelve years earlier, in Jim Mandrell's class on the translator's art, at Indiana University, Bloomington. Now, two hours south of Bloomington, just outside of Leopold where I had been teaching at a rural junior-senior high school, I was determined to get back in earnest to the task that circumstances — finishing a bachelor's degree and teacher certification, being a husband and father, launching my pedagogical career, writing some original stories and essays — had for too long kept me from. I had, indeed, translated about a third of the book, first at breakneck speed in a fairly rough draft and then, painstakingly, in consultation and revision. At last, confident that what I had was worthy of consideration by any university press with an interest in Latin American works in translation, I was set to submit a proposal and begin the final push. But first, it occurred to me, I should check the Internet once more for any English-language translations that I might have missed.

And there they were, hot off the press that very year: *A Visit to the Ranquel Indians*, translated by Eva Gillies, University of Nebraska Press; *An Expedition to the Ranquel Indians*, translated by Mark McCaffrey, University of Texas Press. The original, Lucio V. Mansilla's *Una excursión a*

[1] Previously published in two online magazines: originally, in *New Works Review* (June 2004); then, by the editor's invitation, in *River Walk Journal* (November / December 2004). The present text is slightly edited.

los indios ranqueles, first published in serial form in 1870, had not previously seen print in English since a nineteenth-century edition vaguely alluded to (I have been unable to locate it) by one of Mansilla's commentators. One of those, in an introduction to one of countless Spanish-language editions, ranks the *Excursion* beside José Hernández's *El gaucho Martín Fierro* and Domingo F. Sarmiento's *Facundo* in a triumvirate of outstanding works of Argentine literature of that century. As a first-time translator, then, unconnected and without advanced academic credentials, I had counted on both its obscurity and its renown to catapult me into the realm of literary translators (like the formidable García Márquez's own Gregory Rabassa) that even a celebrated living writer might consider working with. Instead, anguished, looking into the magic mirror of that computer monitor, I saw my own illusions and all of my labor mocked by those two fresh editions that were suddenly, coincidentally, tauntingly available for purchase (and which I did purchase).

I had missed my chance! Had I only persisted earlier, more determinedly, untiringly, I might have beat them by half a decade!

In retrospect, I am glad they beat me. At the time, though, my first reaction was to cry. I drove the twenty minutes from county library to my home and immediately cranked up the old push lawnmower and tore into the better than an acre of unruly country grass that I was then responsible for mowing. By the time I finished, I had worked out a more positive spin on things. If I was not meant to translate Mansilla, I told myself, at least I could not have chosen a better book on which to cut my translator's teeth. And meanwhile, through all of my related readings and researches, surely I was finally ready to write the original story that I had been carrying around in my head for almost twenty years, since I first encountered its seed in a folk song sung by the incomparable Mercedes Sosa, lyrics written by the poet-historian Félix Luna, whose source the blurb on the LP mistakenly said was Mansilla's *Excursion*. (The Spanish-language text and my English translation appear at the beginning of this book.)

Actually, I had completed more than one book-length manuscript by that time. My South American experience was at the heart of both of them. The first, consisting of a novella and related stories tied to a mythical town (like García Márquez's Macondo) called Magdalena, attempted to weave the inward secrets of my sojourn as a Mormon missionary into a magical-realist tapestry of worldly and spiritual significance. A Utah-based editor expressed interest in the book but ultimately passed on it (even after my most earnest attempt at a re-write) because of obvious flaws occasioned in part by my still being too close to the religious experiences that had engendered it. Thank God that, except for one of its stories, which was published in an undergraduate journal at IU called *Labyrinth* (my first publication except for a number of youthful newspaper articles), it was rejected.

The second manuscript, more intimately tied to both Mansilla's book and to that original story that I would turn to now in the summer of '97, was a curious combination of translations and commentary that I called *The Red Flamingo: Gaucho Myths and Legends*. Represented among the translations were two by Mansilla (one I had originally translated in Mandrell's class), two by early twentieth-century writer Ricardo Güiraldes, and excerpts from a couple of crucial episodes of Hernández's nineteenth-century narrative poem. I introduced each section with a brief author biography, and the whole by an approximately hundred-page literary-historical essay (one chapter of which would be published in the Chicano-Riqueño Studies journal *Chiricú*) that attempted to set the literary selections in context. The book was intended for a secondary-school or university audience, and at the suggestion of one professor included pedagogical materials, such as suggestions for study-discussion questions and short essays. In any case, while several publishers said kind things about the manuscript, no one took it on. In the end I decided that the introductory package had been a bit over-ambitious for the accompanying text and might itself have made it a difficult sell.

That particular effort, though, in conjunction with my larger effort with the *Excursion*, had prepared me for that other story that surely I alone was born to write. After I came in from mowing the lawn, showered, and ate dinner, I sat down and began outlining what I would tentatively call *Dorotea of the Pampas*. The first draft, which would be finished when school started in the fall, would weigh in at some hundred and seventy manuscript pages: about 40,000 words.

First, between outlining and writing, I would spend some additional research time at the university library in Bloomington, and at home reading some texts (like the Inca Garcilaso de la Vega's *Comentarios reales de los Incas*) that I had not yet gotten around to. While the central story would concern a young Argentine woman, captured by Indians in the late nineteenth-century, later resisting her rescue by civilization's army, my plan was to create a much broader scene out of some combination of the *Quixote* and the *Excursion*. In Cervantes's book, in the more free-spirited first part, the knight and his squire ended up twice in one particular inn, where the knight's story took a rest while other people's only apparently unrelated (and lengthy) tales were inserted. In Mansilla's book it was around the soldiers' campfire, or among the Indians' tents, that others' tales were related either briefly or at equally sustained length. In imitation of those literary examples, I had long envisioned a gathering at some campfire, on the way out of Indian country, where the captive would tell her life story and again plead her case for the freedom to stay where she no longer felt captive; and, between beginning and end of her tale, a profusion of other stories would be tossed out at the same fire by countless other speakers.

Those other speakers' tales were what required the most study, and what prompted my many-years' hesitation before the daunting task of writing. Those and the simple necessity of inventing a scenario that would be both geographically and socially credible. Mansilla's book, in combination with Hernández's and Güiraldes's, and even Sarmiento's, had gone a long way to preparing me to write about Dorotea, but I also wanted to do much more. Through the Inca Garcilaso's mythical history of his Indian forebears, for instance, I would insert yet another perspective on the tale's central concern with such basic questions as freedom, love, and solitude. One's freedom, after all, might be another's enslavement, yet the enslavement of other native peoples to the Inca lords was considered a blessed freedom, according to the narrative of that son of a Spanish conquistador and Inca princess. Likewise, the freedom that Buenos Aires's Europeanizing elite were fighting for was not the same one that would from time to time inflame the gauchos and other rabble along that cosmopolitan center's savage periphery — as the Iraqi liberation our nation would seek after 9/11 may not be the same one desired by a majority of Iraqis.

Again, the manuscript was occasionally well commented on by different editors. And one literary agent suggested that I send it to a book doctor, who for the price of more than a teacher's monthly take-home salary would deliver a product that might or might not find a publisher. What really got things rolling for me, however, was when I finally decided to do one other thing in response to the apparent disaster of being beaten out in the race to translate Mansilla. I decided to write a letter of introduction to both of those translators. With the letters, I enclosed a copy of my self-published chapbook of prose poems called *Quixotics*. In conjunction with the letters themselves, the chapbook (which had sold perhaps a couple dozen copies, and contained the core idea of the larger story in a paragraph entitled "Dorotea Bazán") was sufficient to charm them both into critiquing my present manuscript. Writing those letters, within a literary context at least, was the most inspired thing I had ever done.

Eva Gillies, born in Germany of a German father and an Argentine-German-Jewish mother, raised in Buenos Aires after the rise of Hitler and educated in England after the rise of Perón, subsequently citizen of the world, was the first to respond with an extremely gracious letter. Mark McCaffrey responded later, a bit more skeptically, but also kindly, persuaded by my chapbook that the other manuscript could not be too bad. So I sent them both a copy and waited. The verdict, in both cases, was that the story was too weighted down with the superfluous others, that I was demanding a bit too much of my reader. Mark, who was particularly brutal with the text, told me that "a lot of the air went out of the soufflé" when he realized that I was approaching the antiquated literary stylings, not with a sense of irony, but with all seriousness, almost worshipfulness. That is where he helped me the most. He forced me to take a cold look at my illusions and to bring a more twenty-first-century literary sensibility and focus to this re-envisioning of a historical past. Eva, for her part, dear friend and confidante that she quickly became, continues to read both my fiction and essays, and is largely responsible for my little Borgesian tale "History of the Knight and the Sophist" becoming the much refined piece that was eventually accepted for publication in *The Journal of Graduate Liberal Studies*.

The year of these new correspondences was 2000. I came out in 2001 with a drastic revision, considerably shorter than the first, and finally, a year later, with the draft (closer to ninety-manuscript pages and 18,000 words) that finally stuck. It had a new title, "A Bride Called Freedom," from a line from a folk song by Argentine poet, singer, and guitarist Atahualpa Yupanqui (the pseudonym borrowed from two Inca kings): "*Yo tengo tantos hermanos que no los puedo contar / y una novia hermosa que se llama libertad*" (I have so many brothers and sisters that I can't count them / and a beautiful bride who's called freedom).

In the middle version, alternatively re-titled "Captive Dorotea" or "La Verde," after the pond where Dorotea's story is related (a paragraph describing that pond was published in the diminutive journal *Paragraph*), I had cut out the most egregious of the inserted tales and added (as had already been present in other of my fictions) some postmodernist narrative touches. In the final version, after first chopping all but one of the remaining interpolations (and even it I greatly abbreviated, subordinating it to the voice of a skeptical interpreter), I spent a bit more time working on the authenticity of Dorotea's rustic voice and on the packaging for a young adult readership. This had been my original intention for the story, though I had mixed feelings. In the end, I suppose, I find those marketing distinctions a bit artificial, anyway, and hope that (like *Huckleberry Finn*, which some people would call a young adult novel) this story will appeal also to an older audience. Certainly, though I have clipped some of the more extended sentences, and in some cases preferred a simpler word to a more obscure one, I have still written for the more literate end of that marketing category, and have been at considerable pains to maintain a rich, varied vocabulary including such favorites as "loquacious," which a middle-aged and well-accomplished educator of my recent acquaintance once admitted to having had to look up. At the same time, I was at pains to shape a layered narrative structure with something of an air of sophistication, of a postmodernist flair that nevertheless encloses a Romantic sentiment. It is like nothing he has ever read, Mark McCaffrey told me, which to my ears sounded something like a compliment.

In the spring of 2003, this much-revised manuscript was tentatively accepted by the bilingual, print-on-demand publisher Ediciones Nuevo Espacio (ENE).[2] I had pitched

2 This publisher has since discontinued its fiction line and is specializing in textbooks.

it as a bilingual book (they also publish single-language books in either Spanish or English); if they agreed, I would have the text translated for me into Spanish. It was thanks in part to Eva Gillies, who introduced me to the Buenos Aires-based writer María Rosa Lojo, that I was able quickly, after ENE's acceptance of that proposal, to put myself in contact with Sebastián R. Bekes, also an Argentine, who lives in the province of Entre Ríos. María Rosa referred me to him. Our collaboration via electronic mail was a remarkable experience for me. Without him, I see no way that I could have produced a Spanish text that would have as accurately reflected both the regional and period idioms. The text as finally accepted was published in November 2003 as *A Bride Called Freedom / Una novia llamada libertad.*

Subsequently, I find myself working on some of Sebastián's Spanish-language stories. Already I had been busy with a couple of María Rosa's books of delicately literate historical fiction (including a set of stories that contains the tale of one Dorotea Cabral, possibly the true historical source of my more loosely imagined character); I have also translated a collection of her prose poems, several of which have already appeared or are forthcoming in literary journals, for the first time in English. These translations have benefited immensely from her own and especially from Eva's critiques. I am currently seeking a publisher for the book of poetry.[3]

3 This book was published in 2008 in a bilingual edition by Host Publications: *Awaiting the Green Morning* (*Esperan la mañana verde*). Later appeared *Passionate Nomads* (Aliform Publishing, 2011), my translation of her historical fantasy novel *Una pasión de los nómades*, with its own association with Mansilla and his book about the Ranquel Indians.

What irks me about all of this is that I chose to live for so many years in something like literary isolation. Yes, I had surrounded myself with a few literary-minded friends who provided some valuable critiques. Yes, I had submitted to many editors, even received a few individualized responses. Yes, I had studied, in fiction-writing workshops, under a couple of professors and writers at the university, as well as under Jim Mandrell in his translation course. But the only times I had ever written a letter to a living writer whose work I admired, I had been sure to say that, if he were too busy, he need not feel any pressure to answer me. And my naturally depressive nature, aided by geographical isolation if nothing else, delayed many collaborations and progress that might otherwise have occurred much sooner.

Whereas now, by virtue of two letters to the living translators who I first thought had stolen my hope, two letters that dared to invite them into the world of my own imaginative endeavors, thanks to that simple determination, my creative life is vastly rejuvenated, my progress comparably accelerated; and more importantly, perhaps, the circle of my friends and acquaintances expanded.

Mark Barrett, a Benedictine monk of the Worth Abbey in Sussex, England, in his book *Crossings* that Eva once sent me in answer to my own vacillations regarding religious faith, says this: "that the moment one definitely commits oneself, then providence moves too" (London: Darton, Longman & Todd, 2001, p. 47).

The American writer Carolyn See, in her book *Making a Literary Life* (Random House, 2002), admonishes every aspirant to write one "charming note" to a different writer or editor every day, without asking a favor. Some of those writers and editors, she suggests, might even write back.

I have not gotten around to writing one of those notes every day — I doubt, anyway, that such a practice (plus the requisite thousand words daily of new writing, or comparable amount of editing) is possible to sustain throughout a secondary-school teacher's, writer's, and family-man's full twelve-month calendar — but I have begun to write an occasional letter of the sort, and I hope thereby to acquire even a few more friends and amiable critics of my work. It does seem clear to me, above all, that Mark Barrett was right: surely a sort of providence began moving for me once I definitely committed myself, through those two letters, to a further immersion in the literary life.

Justifying Viviana:
A Literary-Rhetorical Argument

Why, I have been asked, if Dorotea Bazán is the real protagonist in my historical romance of the Argentine pampas, did I invent Viviana Suárez? How, in other words, do I justify her existence when all I needed to do was set Dorotea down beside the pond called La Verde and allow her to tell her story? What need of Viviana, with her occasionally snarky comments, stage-directing her invisible friend Elizabeth through Dorotea's paces?

The question is good and deserves, I think, a public accounting.

The short of it is that Viviana lives so that Dorotea herself might more fully live in our hearts and minds. I wish her to be not just alive in the context of that world so distant to us that it might almost seem a world of make-believe, but more profoundly alive in the context of this universe of countervailing joys and sorrows that we inhabit in the twenty-first century. I want her to be more evidently pertinent to our own times and circumstances. I want the *readers*, that is, to meet Dorotea actively enough that they look at present affairs with different or, at least, more attentive eyes. For it is one thing to read, over an evening or two, about something faraway and almost as quickly forgotten, but quite another to come awake to how the things that we are reading about actually pertain to us in the here and now.

In the case of Dorotea's story, Viviana helps me in a few ways. First, by her youthful exuberance and irreverence before the almost "ancient" (and therefore "sacred") text, she provides a corrective to its prejudices and blind spots: this is particularly evident in the instance of her mocking of the overtly anti-Indian poem of Esteban Echeverría, one of the fathers of Argentine literature whose modest contribution is otherwise not without its merits.

A second way is that she allows me access to Mansilla's own words, from the book that he wrote about the Ranquel Indians. His book is still read and remains important today because in 1870 his was almost the only voice, in the young nation's literary or political spheres, to question the official verities of his civilization and recognize a parallel humanity in people the nation tended to see only as savages — as *animals*. Every word and thought attributed to Mansilla in "A Bride Called Freedom" — everything except for some contextually necessary small talk — come directly from the *Excursion*.

Likewise, aside from her own youthful enthusiasm and the prophetic voice of Mansilla, Viviana also allows me access to a wonderful account from the early seventeenth-century Spanish novelist Miguel de Cervantes's brilliant *The Adventures of Don Quixote of La Mancha*. The story that I speak of is that of the beautiful shepherdess Marcela. In her own feminist speech of female agency, she eloquently explains that she does not want to marry and has taken to the surrounding fields to avoid so many importunate suitors. When Viviana has Colonel Mansilla rise up at novella's end and, by threat of sword, stop the captain from preventing Dorotea's return to her Indian husband and children, Mansilla is re-enacting the mad knight's own action to prevent suitors and friends of suitors from following Marcela.

The text of "A Bride Called Freedom," as edited for this edition, does not actually contain any direct allusion to Marcela, as the first edition did. But Marcela is there, subliminally, in the substance of Dorotea's speech. Marcela's voice comes across most directly in the fourth and final of those concluding fragments. Dorotea says: "I was born a free being. To live free, I chose the loneliness of these pampas. These pampas are where I want to stay, where my soul always will …" Marcela, as I translate: "I was born free, and in order to live free I chose these fields: the trees of these mountains are my companions; the clear waters of these creeks, my mirrors. . . ." It is this insistence on feminine free will — which runs from beginning to end of Dorotea's larger narrative itself and pervades each of these "invented" fragments — that sustains the allusion.

To call Marcela (or Cervantes himself, as some have suggested) a feminist because of this may be a bit of an anachronism, but his attitude toward the free will of both his male and female characters is notable. It may be no less anachronistic, then, for Viviana to invent a Dorotea who is in some truly modern sense a feminist. Who can question, after all, that captive women in those days, as well as in ours, have resented and sometimes struggled against the restraints put upon them by a patriarchal society? The literary distortion, then, functions to bring our fictitious heroine into our presence, making her all the more current to us.

Through all of this, however, it is never my intention to dismiss or disparage the traditional form of the historical romance itself, any more than it was Cervantes's intention to heap everlasting dishonor on the chivalric romance, as many have mis- (or over-) interpreted. Viviana, after all, promises her friend Elizabeth “the full revelation of the romance” and, in the end, closes “with heart aflutter.” The snarky intrusions serve, ultimately, to sharpen the modern feel and credibility of the romance.

Which is not to say that a similar effect might not have been obtained by other means. A prominent example of a novel that did is Thornton Wilder’s acclaimed *The Bridge of San Luis Rey* (1927). At the suggestion of Mansilla-translator Mark McCaffrey, I read it in preparation for the revision of the bulkier and more traditionally-structured original draft of what would become “A Bride Called Freedom.”

Wilder’s novel’s complex narrative is based on the intersecting lives of five people who died, early in the eighteenth century, with the collapse of an Incan rope bridge across the Apurímac River (a geographical location, incidentally, that figures in the mythology at center of my Dorotea narrative’s companion story, “The Prince and His Father”). Wilder’s fiction, narrated in the third person by an ironic, early twentieth-century voice, centers on the Franciscan friar, Father Juniper’s, investigation into the lives of those five deceased, with the intention of proving God’s justice (in punishing the wicked) and mercy (in bringing the righteous swiftly to heaven).

Another example is Manuel Mujica Lainez’s *The Wandering Unicorn* (1965). It is narrated by the world-weary and sarcastic Melusine, half-woman and half-fairy whose present and intolerable immortality is the indirect result of an earlier transgression — punished by the witch-mother whose wishes Melusine and her sister thought they were carrying out.

Dorotea, for her part, while certainly an intelligent and perceptive woman, is not, like Melusine, centuries old, cosmopolitan, and vastly experienced in both physical and magical realms. Her experience is limited; as she tells her story, she is fewer than twenty years old and has no knowledge of the twentieth, let alone twenty-first century. Given that fact, and that I wanted Dorotea's story to be related, essentially, in her own words, the expansive perspective of these examples seemed unavailable to me. For as much as I might have preferred to stick with the simpler approach that is outlined in this essay's first paragraph — as I did in the original draft — I had to resort to some contrivance.

So I spent several months to a year dreaming up something resembling the solution that I ultimately chose. The details that were worked out, in the writing and re-writing, rely upon a framing voice not as remote as Wilder's semi-omniscient narrator's (who never introduces himself and may or may not be the author) but one more intimately involved in the story as it unfolds. Viviana, in assuming that role, becomes something of a puppeteer, moving characters around, pulling strings and interpreting as she goes, but guided — always guided — by Dorotea's voice that she enlivens. Viviana, in other words, unlike Melusine who is present in and living the story she tells, is outside looking in, but simultaneously breathing life into the character that guides her. By that stratagem, our twice-captive heroine is able to speak from across the abyss that otherwise separates us.

However much my novella might be considered a sort of postmodernist invention, though, the centuries hold plenty of other examples of the story-within-the-story or of the story as discovered manuscript. Most pertinent to the present case are strategies such as Cervantes uses, not so much to bring the past into focus in a modern context, but to bring a richer profusion of perspectives to bear on the problems of his own and his readers' age.

In this context of bringing a diversity of perspectives and realities — present and historical — together to illuminate the literary text, I have considered chapter seven the thematic center of "A Bride Called Freedom." In early drafts, a great many other voices spoke at the Mansillan campfire, each bearing a particular experience and point of view on the larger theme of freedoms, captivities, and solitudes in this American hemisphere, more particularly in the South. In a later aside, the connection is explicitly drawn between Argentina's war of extermination against the pampean Indians and the one taking place at roughly the same time in the vast Western territories of our North American manifest destiny. But there in chapter seven, Echeverría's prejudicial view of civilization and barbarism pushes out all the extraneous voices — extraneous to Dorotea's particular tale — and then, against Captain Rivadavia's passionate complaint, the other men and women already gathered at that fire have their say on the so-called "Indian question." In the end, one perspective — Dorotea's — is favored, but it is a bittersweet victory, given the dramatic irony of what we know (and Dorotea and her husband sense) about the larger history that has yet to play out.

My justification of Viviana, then, with which this essay begins, stretches beyond the confines of the original novella to form a bridge from that pampean legend to the Incan myth of Viracocha or Pachacutec, which was the most important of those superfluous campfire narratives that hit the chopping block. The paradox of individual freedom and freedom within community is present in Dorotea's life with the Ranquel, where she comes to feel more at home than she ever did among her own people, on that ill-defined and nebulous frontier between proper Buenos Aires society and the barbarism of Indian life. But the paradox is more sharply defined in the Incan tale, in which that indigenous empire — in the mists of its own history — is, like the Spaniards' empire, a supposedly benevolent civilizer of savage peoples: or "Indians," as the Christianized Inca Garcilaso also calls the subjects of his royal ancestors.

Modern historians will question that implicit benevolence of the Incan Empire, just as numerous voices question that of the American Empire whose legs, both economically and militarily, currently straddle much of the globe. In "The Prince and His Father" we are concerned primarily with the human story, with its necessary element of ancestral and personal myth, though all the injustices and turmoil that we are familiar with in this present world are reflected in what we see of Pacha's struggle.

Viviana, for her part, at somewhat more than a decade and a half after the adolescent girl we first met through her voice alone, tells us about the proud and rebellious king Hancohuallu, who cannot bear to be subject to another, and so crosses the mountains with those of his former subjects who will follow. His story rubs against the imperial tale of divine benevolence, but so does the conflict between old Bloody Tears — who is certainly less than generous toward his son — and the once-rebellious prince who rises to his higher nature and ascends to the place of Inca lord.

Appearances deceive; perspectives clash; realities and points of view appear remarkably fluid, even among the gods' divinely anointed.

"*There are so many different freedoms*," Pacha muses as his mother begins to wind down that tale. "*It's almost like, if you're free, someone else has to be a slave.*"

And Viviana, reflecting on "the enigmatic figure of Atahualpa, whom Pizarro and his Spanish troops captured and cruelly executed," considers him (despite Garcilaso's dismissing him as a mere pretender to the Incan throne) "a fitting symbol of that whole magnificent empire that, with his betrayal and death, came abruptly to an end" — and whose paradoxical "lessons of community and liberty, each intertwined and dependent on the other," she continually ponders.

And here we cross over (or circle back) to our own world, from which Viviana's voice first crossed onto Dorotea's Argentine pampa. Our metaphorical prince finds himself on a tenuous thread of possibility, his battle really just begun, but the hope and the potential of a triumphant future foreshadowed. And in his case, unlike his mythic forebears', the physical father is carrying him. The struggle is shared.

But pointing the way (or, like the Pachamama, gathering in) is wife and mother. It is not insignificant that we read, at the end of this long story, that "a woman would lead them." The significance of that emblematic statement is all the greater if we imagine that, beside Viviana, must invariably stand Dorotea. Each gives breath and takes life from the other, each with her "hair aglow beneath a nimbus of moonlight" — each, in her essential narrative function (or functions), fully justified.

Attractions of Barbarism,

or, Dreaming a Complete Argentina[1]

My home since late Monday was on the ninth floor of an apartment building at 1744 Gascón where it formed a diagonal with Aráoz and Scalabrini Ortiz, neatly dissecting the city block between Nicaragua and Soler. It was an ordinary and modest high-rise with two accordion-door elevators. The ninth floor had two apartment suites. The Luba Tango Guest House, where I was staying, occupied suite B.

María Rosa Lojo and her husband Oscar Beuter were there to pick me up at just after noon on Saturday. She rang from downstairs and I appeared with my packed bags. The boarding house's Russian immigrant owner, Luba, would hold my room for Sunday evening or Monday — just better than a week later — when I planned to be back in Old Palermo.

I recognized Oscar from a photograph (more than a decade old) of the two of them and their first two children beside Oscar's refurbished antique Mercedes. The picture had accompanied an article about her 1994 novel *La pasión de los nómades* and the family's investigative journey that

1 Drawn and adapted from scattered passages in my as-yet unpublished travel memoir, *Journeys and Digressions*, this essay – under the title "Attractions of Barbarity" – was the winner of a runner-up prize in the 2015 X.J. Kennedy Award and appeared in issue #60 of *Rosebud*. As for my back-and-forth between *barbarism* and *barbarity*, I am persuaded back to my original usage in "A Bride Called Freedom" for the sake of consistency with that novella and with other English-language translations of South American literature, as well as by more intricate and decisive linguistic factors.

preceded it — retracing as best as possible, at a century's remove, Lucio V. Mansilla's steps into the heart of what in 1870 was still Ranquel Indian country.

Mansilla, indirectly, through his classic account of that journey called *Una excursión a los indios ranqueles*, was responsible for my being there on this, my second Argentine adventure. To be brief, by means of what became my historical novella *A Bride Called Freedom* (2003), in which Mansilla is a character, I had come to be working on a translation of María Rosa's novel (*Passionate Nomads*, 2011), and I was invited to read, from Sebastián Bekes's Spanish-language translation of my fiction, at a conference in the name of Mansilla and his sister Eduarda to be convened on July 1 and 2, 2005 in the colonial city of Córdoba.

The drive to the Buenos Aires suburb of Castelar took just under an hour. When we pulled up in front of the house, Oscar let us out and opened the gate. We followed, approaching the house on a stone walkway that cut through the small lawn. Twenty-two-year-old Leonor was standing just outside the door, sporting a colorful youthful outfit and a welcoming smile. Inside, I met Federico, twelve; and later that evening Alfonso, twenty-four, a musician with a vaguely bohemian air.

The house, inside and out, was beautiful and elegant in the modest Spanish style. It was the same house which María Rosa's father had built for his family, in which she grew up the "exiled daughter" of a Republican partisan in Spain's civil war, living in the shadow of the mythical Galician landscape of his memory and imagination as represented tangibly by a chestnut tree he planted in the back yard. Though, outside of its natural environment, it never produced edible fruit, it only died after his death and after María Rosa's "return" to the green territory of a Spanish Galicia she had never seen except through his eyes — as if "it had simply fulfilled its earthly mission" (as she writes in her "Minimal Autobiography"), "that it had always been there only to embody the force of desire, the powerful throbbing of nostalgia, the first commandment imposed on the exiled child."

It was that same house, anyway, though the tree was gone and Oscar and María Rosa had built onto it. When I entered into my first correspondence with her it was covered with tarp, their planned remodeling held captive by the economic collapse of 2001, because no one could access the money they had placed in banks: consequently, they could not pay the laborers to continue their work. During this period, there were terrible sufferings among the general populace and an unprecedented succession of interim presidents. There were protests and rushes on food. Local currencies arose and communities established systems of barter and mutual help. The nation had still not recovered, despite the relative stability of Néstor Kirchner's current presidency which eventually took hold.

In her novel *Anne Frank Is Argentine*, Marisa Presti writes movingly of this period of time, though the central emotional struggle of her narrative is tied to events that had transpired over twenty years earlier during the generals' infamous "dirty war" against its own population. In those days, thousands of citizens disappeared into secret prisons, sites of torture and brutality that in the novel are compared to the concentration camps of Nazi Germany. Presti, aside from a psychological portrait of her country two decades later, offers a critique of Argentine journalism that coincides perfectly with East European journalist Riszard Kapuscinski's observation that I had just read in the current issue of the literary-cultural magazine *Ñ*: "I believe that there is a false interpretation of the Anglo-Saxon tradition of objectivity, because that notion was created from another root which said that the so-called 'fourth power' had to be objective in the face of the activities of other powers (judicial, executive, etc.). But it was never thought of in terms of objectivity in the face of injustice, in the face of the evils that encircle our humanity and make our lives hard. One cannot be objective in the face of torture and dictatorship, that is inhuman."

If Presti's journalistic protagonist and narrator is right, his own profession's present dysfunction may all be caused by the evils of that earlier time, about which Argentina remained sharply divided. Be that as it may (the argument begs the question of that relatively recent tragedy's deeper historical roots), it is the novel's present moment that interests me here. Our protagonist, at this point, has just been reading the morning paper. "The country's stage seemed surreal," Presti writes from his perspective, "as if what was happening were part of a nightmare. Something deep inside wouldn't let you believe it was real. How could you digest the fact that a group of people, hungry in the extreme and armed with knives and long-bladed daggers, had killed and quartered young bulls from a ranch truck that had overturned on the highway, carrying away with them, amidst fighting, enormous pieces of the animals slung over their backs. It was difficult to assimilate this fact as true." Yet this is no flight of Presti's authorial fancy; I remember reading similar reports at the time in the international section of a U.S. newspaper.

~*~

Leonor was a student of *las artes plásticas*. When I asked her if she had any samples of her work at home, she brought me a few loose watercolors and a stack of sketchbooks. Her artistic sense was unique, intriguing. I found myself a bit disoriented at first, trying to establish the nature of the "reality" I saw reflected before me. Yet the connection to real images was always there, like a word that remains forever on the tip of one's tongue, at once perceptible and inexpressible.

As far as I had glimpsed it, Leonor's art was of the sort that makes the viewer take hold of the bits of reality that are presented and piece them back together in a sort of creative collaboration with the artist. I was reminded (with the vague imprecision of a generalist) of the major revolutions of the 20th century art world: the Cubist art of Spaniard Pablo Picasso; the Surrealist creations of his compatriot (the Catalonian) Salvador Dalí. The period that spanned the two world wars was characterized especially, in both plastic and literary arts, by an increasing fragmentation of reality. The startling reality-shattering juxtapositions of Ultraistic images, embodied in Argentina in the work of Jorge Luis Borges and Ricardo Güiraldes, replaced idealized Modernist images. Which is not to say, simplistically, that Leonor Beuter Lojo's art was derived from her predecessors the Cubists, the Surrealists, and the Ultraists but just to give, without the pictures themselves, a way of thinking about them.

I was perhaps most intrigued among the larger quantity of Leonor's sketches with the image — variously repeated and revisited — of a bull tied up by rope, beside or above it the legend: "Cellar of the Bound Bull." I thought it a mere whim of the artist's and briefly wondered about its origins. Only later that night would I be reminded of the tale, which María Rosa's and my mutual friend Eva Gillies (translator of Mansilla) had once told me, of the actual Bodega del Toro Atado.

This bodega was Oscar's wine cellar. Aside from his daily labors as an engineer and his practical-creative handiwork around the house (remodeling the aforementioned antique Mercedes; building, later, entirely from scrapped parts, a travel trailer to pull behind it), Oscar made his own wines. The name was immortalized on the wooden sign — a gift from María Rosa's father and Eva's husband Mick, both now deceased — that greeted all visitors to the cellar. The history behind that legend had to do with an old family joke with its basis in an Argentine idiom in which, when things are going exceptionally well, one speaks not of having "a cat by the tail," as we might in American English, but a roped or bound cow; when on one occasion María Rosa chanced to use the expression in reference to herself, Oscar, the still smitten lover, archly replied that no, it was the *bull* that she had all tied in knots. Suddenly I understood the look of contented and serene drunkenness on the face of the willingly bound bull of Leonor's drawings.

~*~

On Sunday afternoon María Rosa, Oscar, Federico, and I piled into the newer of their two cars, the one that had picked me up the previous day, and headed for the proverbial *Feria de Mataderos*, a fair that takes place on every Sunday and includes everything from performers on horses to singers of tangos and demonstrations of indigenous craftsmanship and dance. The flea market of traditional goods and crafts was as immense as the throng of people that jostled each other to walk through it. The closest I had seen for sheer variety and native spectacle was a North American Indian powwow, though it also contained elements of our county fairs and Western rodeos.

Mataderos merits a substantial mention in Álvaro Abós's literary guide to Buenos Aires — *Al pie de la letra*, or roughly: *Footnotes* — by virtue of its indirect association (for it did not exist as such at the time) with the sanguineous subject matter of Esteban Echeverría's polemical short story "*El matadero*," written between 1838 and 1840 and published posthumously three decades later. A *matadero* is a slaughterhouse, bloody site of the butchering of cattle. *Mataderos* was such a place in its heyday, but in Echeverría's day Buenos Aires's slaughterhouses were all located elsewhere. Still, it affords Abós the excuse to mention that vitriolic allegory in which the whole of Federalist Buenos Aires, in the lamentable times (through the 1830s and '40s) of Mansilla's uncle Juan Manuel de Rosas's dictatorship, becomes a slaughterhouse for the "savage Unitarists" of Rosas's political opposition.

In his essay "Seven Plates of Rice Pudding," Mansilla relates the story of his encounter with him as a boy not yet twenty years old. After hearing, while abroad in London, the ominous tale of the "mad traitor" and "savage Unitarist" Urquiza's uprising against him, Mansilla rushed home at once, his political understanding of the nature of Rosas's governance not yet matured, and went the day after his arrival to call on him in the splendor of that old Palermo that no longer properly exists. Rosas kept him waiting until quite late at night, while Mansilla — conscious of his mother's awaiting him for dinner — declined all invitations to eat with his cousin Manuelita and those others there gathered. Finally summoned to see him, Mansilla was presented with a voluminous "Message" which in all patriarchal arrogance Rosas proceeded to read to him. But he didn't read far before asking his nephew if he was hungry, inviting him to a plate of that famous and mouth-watering *arroz con leche*.

As the reading continued to drag on, the plates continued to come, gigantic plates, as was the custom in Palermo and particularly in that house, plate after plate even after Mansilla had protested that the second or third was quite enough, until, when he had finished his seventh and his stomach was fit to burst, Rosas finally handed him the mammoth anti-Unitarist diatribe he had been reading from and urged his nephew to finish it at home. This darkly comical incident becomes macabre when Mansilla and his father visit Rosas later in his English exile and he reminds them of the incident; with the exact words of Mansilla's father to his mother ("Didn't I tell you your brother is mad?"), spoken afterwards in private were it not, apparently, for the listening ears of one of Rosas's domestic spies, their own servant.

In Abós's book he refers to *Mataderos* as "*el* far west *de Buenos Aires*," the place where city meets the pampas upon which it was erected. Echeverría is not the only writer he evokes; there were others who wrote, like Carl Sandburg of his own boisterous Chicago, of the place itself. And this last allusion is not a careless one: Mataderos's industrial zone was once called Chicago; one of its streets still is, and New — or Nuevo — Chicago the name of its thriving nightclub. Sandburg's Chicago was, like Mataderos, a rugged place well worthy of the scathing pen of Upton Sinclair, who, in *The Jungle,* declaimed against the filth and inhuman squalor of the city's slaughterhouses and meat-packing industry where its largely immigrant population inevitably grunted, sickened, and died.

~*~

Gray skies and a light mist greeted me on the inaugural morning of Mansilla's historical-literary congress on Friday, July 1. I had been in Córdoba since early Monday morning in order to explore the city on my own and visit with friends met on my original Argentine journey in 1979. I hailed a taxi, anyway, found the building at Belgrano 224, and met up again with María Rosa and then Eva Gillies, who had flown in from her home in England.

The topic of María Rosa's keynote address was "The Mansilla Siblings: Beyond Dichotomous Thought or How One Writes a Complete Argentina." The first thing to be said about her presentation is the amazing scope and the incisive intellect behind it; yet her style of presentation was relaxed and conversational, its effect sort of like that of a superlative classroom lecture by a great university professor, upon whose every word and inflection of voice her most ardent disciples hang.

The principal dichotomy of María Rosa's title is the civilization vs. barbarism theme of late 19th century president Domingo F. Sarmiento's anti-Federalist *Facundo*, an account based on the life and death of an (in)famous gaucho leader, or caudillo, named Juan Facundo Quiroga; of Esteban Echeverría's anti-Indian narrative poem "*La cautiva*" ("The Captive") and his already-cited prose allegory of political savagery; of José Mármol's tragic heroine, in his novel *Amalia*, who is destroyed by that merciless bloodletting — in other words, of pretty much everything that was written in those days by anyone other than Mansilla and his sister, whose novel, *Pablo, or Life on the Pampas,* was as comprehending of the plight of those others as was her brother's *Excursión.*

The duty of the writer or historian, María Rosa would suggest, is to rescue those beings whose memory has almost been erased; to reflect, as the Mansilla siblings do, that the wildest Indian, for instance, was no less human than the Christians who went among them with malice. Among those to be rescued from the forgetfulness of a one-sided historical record were also women, she added, "the other excluded ones," not only those captive by Indians in that day but the Mothers of the Plaza de Mayo of recent times, at whom people looked and called "crazy women" while in fact they were "humanity's educators." Lucio and Eduarda Mansilla, in María Rosa's considered opinion, were engaged in a public remembering of those voices; in other words, they were attempting to write "a complete Argentina."

After lunch, Eva spoke on the topic of her English-language translation of Mansilla's *Excursión.* Aside from the particular history that brought her to the book, much of which she had told me before in letters, she focused on matters of translation that were particularly problematic. The reality behind the word *algarroba*, for example, was essentially untranslatable, the particular American tree being quite distinct from the Spanish algarroba or carob tree that the new "discoverers" named it for; thus the decision to stick with the Spanish word and attach an endnote. A similar matter occurred with the book's title: *excursión* could be translated as "excursion" or "expedition"; while she would have preferred "excursion," she bowed to her editor's reservations and settled for *A* Visit *to the Ranquel Indians*, more conducive than any alternative she could think of to the only marginally official purposes of Mansilla's actual and memoiristic journeys, relaxed philosophical explorations and meanderings that they were. In any case, she argued, especially in a casual glossing over of botanical details or obscure historical and literary allusions, a lesser precision might make for an accessible text but also a falsified text, not a truly modern rendering but a merely popular one.

She had come to the University of Nebraska Press with her translation when she learned that not only had they heard of Mansilla, as those at Oxford University Press had not, but they were actively seeking a translation of the *Excursión*. When she also heard that they had already rejected one translation for "lack of quality," she said to herself: "Now, these are exactly the kind of snobs that I would like to work with!" The editorial goal, she said, was for "the English Mansilla for all time." For a stylistic model, she ended up with Robert Louis Stevenson the essayist and literary critic, and "one of the most unjustly underestimated writers of English literature"; she had started by looking at James Fenimore Cooper, a seemingly more likely candidate, but whose pompous overly-florid style constituted "a true insult to the prose of our Mansilla."

Following in quick succession were a number of shorter presentations of which mine was second to last. A particularly good one was given later that afternoon by historian and writer María Gabriela Mizraje. Her topic: "Lucio V. Mansilla and the Dream of a Dandy." She spoke with remarkable clarity, sophistication, and radiance about the artful rhythm that Mansilla's narrative achieves through its frequent attention to matters of food and sleep, in particular his facetious dreams of glory whereby he pokes fun at himself and elaborates on the deeper significance of the experience. Between dream and wakefulness, she suggested, lies a type of frontier that in his work becomes the deliberate literary mirror of the physical frontier that he dared to cross with such particular imaginative daring. Feigning that he dreamt, he lived like a man of the pampas; while dreaming, nevertheless, quite like a city dweller. By this process, she suggested, he was advancing not only in space but toward the rhetoric of the Other, thus engaging with it in a way that no one before him had — and thus giving it value.

That is my best paraphrase of what I think was one of the most perceptive and brilliant presentations of either day. I was surprised that a couple of her fellow scholars seemed to object to what she had said, as if she were somehow slandering Mansilla. It strikes me rather that she was saying the same thing as he in an essay about a colorful frontier episode involving the murder of a horse, in response to impatient readers whom he imagined urging him to come quickly to story's end: "Is writing not an art and a game?"

My own reading was as successful as I might have hoped it to be and certainly better than I might have feared. First I briefly reiterated what was already stated in the program's written summary: that the narrator of this passage, one Viviana Suárez, North American daughter of Argentine parents, has been vacationing in Buenos Aires between high school and university and has discovered the old manuscript that pretends, as dictated to Mansilla, to tell the story of Dorotea Bazán, captive of Indians; that now, in one of a series of e-mails to her friend Leeza, with whom she has formerly learned their Spanish teacher's version of the story as he had intuited it strictly from the lyrics of a song, she is setting the stage for Dorotea's voice and inviting her friend to step back with her into that former world of their teacher's partial conjuring.

Then I read from my friend Sebastián's translation, in an unhurried and leisurely voice, the majority of that chapter starting with the description of the verdant pond and ending in an abbreviated account of Mansilla's campfire tale of a muleteer who, fleeing from justice in the days of Juan Facundo Quiroga, got caught by his hair in a tree and ended up eating his shirt and dying of indigestion. Afterwards, stopping at the point of Mansilla's listeners' hurrahs and his vainglorious bow, I simply closed the book and looked up, meeting María Gabriela's expectant eyes. "Is that it?" she asked, and when I answered that it was, everyone applauded. And what a thrill it is to be convincingly applauded!

I say *convincingly* because I have had plenty of occasion to give polite applause to performances that scarcely deserved it. I won't say if I have ever been at the receiving end of such half-hearted recognition. In such cases, as Mansilla himself has observed, one can never be sure that the audience is not applauding the fact that one has finally ceased to perform, so that they can finally go home. In this case, anyway, its genuineness was attested to by the fact of a greater than usual number of questions and not one of them of an even slightly vituperative nature. The "eternal instant" of my fleeting literary triumph, to borrow Borges's phrase, was complete.

About the Author

Brett Alan Sanders is a literary translator, writer, and retired teacher living in Tell City, Indiana. He earned a BA in Spanish from Indiana University and an MALS from the University of Southern Indiana. He has published original fiction and essays as well as translations from Spanish in a number of literary journals in the U.S. and abroad, including essays, in Spanish, at the online journal *Revista Letra Urbana*, and an English-language essay (with Serbo-Croatian translation) in the premiere issue of the Bosnian journal *Hourglass Literary Magazine*. His published books are *A Bride Called Freedom/ Una novia llamada libertad* (Ediciones Nuevo Espacio, 2003), early bilingual edition of the English-language *The Captive and the Prince: Tales of Freedom and Courage* (Per Bastet Publications, 2021), with the revised novella, an additional story, and related essays and nonfiction narrative; the original collection of newspaper essays *Confabulating with the Cows: Wit, Whimsy, and Occasional Wisdom from Perry County, Indiana: 1992-94* (Per Bastet Publications, 2017); two translations from the work of Buenos Aires writer María Rosa Lojo: a bilingual edition of her prose poetry collection *Awaiting the Green Morning* (Host Publications, 2008) and the novel *Passionate Nomads* (Aliform Publishing, 2011); and the bilingual edition of Argentine American author Luis Alberto Ambroggio's tribute to Walt Whitman: *Todos somos Whitman/We Are All Whitman* (Arte Público Press, 2016).
Website: www.brettalansanders.wordpress.com.
Email: brettalansanders@gmail.com.

www.ingramcontent.com/pod-product-compliance
Lightning Source LLC
Chambersburg PA
CBHW061549250926
52052CB00010B/3122